Also by Joyce W. Hahn

California Yankee Under Three Flags
Defeat, Resist and Rescue

VIVA ESPAÑA

Joyce w. Hahn

iUniverse, Inc.
Bloomington

Viva España

iUniverse books may be ordered through booksellers or by contacting:

iUniverse
1663 Liberty Drive
Bloomington, IN 47403
www.iuniverse.com
1-800-Authors (1-800-288-4677)

ISBN: 978-1-4502-8432-5 (pbk)
ISBN: 978-1-4502-8433-2 (ebk)

Printed in the United States of America

iUniverse rev. date: 1/13/2011

For fallen comrades

When the Reds shoot our people their last cry is our cry, 'Viva España'. I have seen several Reds being shot and they too cried at the end, 'Viva España'. (words of a Nationalist, black-shirted pilot)

Arthur Koestler, *Dialogue With Death*

The dead sleep cold in Spain tonight. Snow blows through the olive groves, sifting against the tree roots. Snow drifts over the mounds with small headboards. For our dead are part of the earth of Spain now and the earth of Spain can never die. Each winter it will seem to die and each spring it will come alive again. Our dead will live with it forever.

Ernest Hemingway

ACKNOWLEDGMENTS

I want to thank several people who helped me write this book: Susan Hahn, who suggested the subject of La Pasionaria and her role in the Spanish Civil War, Nina Hahn, who read the manuscript, and to the members of my writing group, Joan Condon, Natalya Dragunsky, George Hahn, Beverly Paik, Evelyn Smart and Nick Souza.

Part I

1

San Francisco
November, 1975

The restaurant bar was thick with tobacco smoke and smelled of spilled wine, garlic and musty woolens. As Meg elbowed her way through the crowd of men at the bar, a breathless waitress rushed toward her. "Franco is dying!"the woman shouted, pointing to the television over the bar. "It's on the news!" Meg stared at the woman, whose round, black eyes shone as if she were in ecstasy. Franco was dying? Meg peered over the heads of the men whose eyes were fixed on the screen. The leather-faced Basque sheepherders were holding up glasses of red wine, laughing and shouting, their noise drowning out the announcer's words.

Meg gave the woman a tight embrace. "At last!"she murmured, tears brimming in her eyes. "I'd heard he was ill, but didn't dare believe he'd ever give up. It's been so long." Meg then remembered her guest, Ellen. She faced the young woman who trailed behind her, staring at her as if she didn't believe what she'd just heard. Meg brushed the tears from her eyes. "You're shocked, I know. Let's sit down. I'll try to explain."

The waitress guided them to a table in the dining room, and as she handed them the menu she said,"Mrs. Howard, I hope you and your friend don't mind the noise. You can understand how we Basques feel—especially these sheepherders down from the Sierra."

"Yes. I truly do." Meg felt a wave of emotion that prevented her from speaking for a moment. She calculated the number of years Franco had been in power. Since 1939. Thirty-six years. She glanced at Ellen who was still watching her with puzzled eyes. "You don't understand. You're too young. The Spanish Civil War happened eons ago."

The waitress brought a carafe of red wine and filled their glasses. Meg lifted her glass in a toast. "Salud," she said, but thinking, may Franco die soon—a hard death.

Ellen responded to the toast and then set down her wine glass. She smiled at Meg. "That war was before my time, but I've seen Picasso's *Guernica* and read my Hemingway and Orwell. I think I *do* understand."

"Of course. It's just that celebrating someone's death seems so ghoulish." Meg pushed a strand of dark hair from her forehead then reached into her bag for her reading glasses. She picked up the menu the waitress had given her. A wild shout came from the bar and all eyes were turned in that direction. Meg waited expectantly, but the shouts subsided to a drunken party-sound. The waitress shook her head as she as she came toward them. "Not yet," she said, her plump cheeks flushed with excitement.

After Meg gave the the waitress the order for roast lamb and salad for them both, she tucked her glasses back in her purse. She smiled at Ellen."Well, instead of talking about Franco, I guess we should get down to business and discuss the Assistant Professorship you've applied for." Meg was a professor in UC Berkeley's Journalism Department. Ellen was a prospective candidate.

Ellen nodded and sipped her wine. "But you said you had something to explain—about the Basques—and Franco? You were there, in Spain, weren't you, during the civil war?"

"Yes, I was." Meg gave a wry laugh. "But it's a complicated subject. Not for the Basques, of course, these Sierra sheepherders. They hate Franco with a burning passion. Not only did he order the carpet bombing and strafing of Guernica's civilian population—a historical first, by the way—he abolished the independent Basque state. No, it's clear why the people here are so euphoric. But I feel I need to explain why I'm so involved."

Ellen smiled and shrugged. "It's not a rare reaction, I'm sure. Franco was a fascist. The Spanish were the first Europeans to fight against fascism. It was the dress rehearsal for World War II."

"Yes. And possibly World War II could have been avoided if it hadn't been for the democracies' betrayal. The Republicans were elected democratically. Franco and his generals launched a right-wing rebellion." Meg's voice was rising. She could feel her cheeks flush with anger. "The Republican militias needed weapons, planes, oil—and the only country to help them was Soviet Russia—which came with strings attached." Meg stopped herself. She touched Ellen's hand. "I'm sorry, Ellen. I'm lecturing. You know all this, of course. It's just that... I witnessed Franco's terror firsthand." She took a sip of wine to calm herself.

Ellen gave Meg a thoughtful look. "How long were you in Spain?"

"From 1936 to '38. In Madrid. Also Barcelona."

"You must have been very young. You don't look old enough to have been there that long ago."

"I was young, 24, a cub reporter. I'm now 63. I'll be retiring soon."

"Amazing." Ellen stared at Meg. "But how did you got such an assignment? Most war correspondents have years of experience under their belts. Only 24! I can't imagine how exciting that must have been for you."

"Indeed." Meg laughed. "Actually, I had a sponsor. A lover. Tom Wells. He was a reporter for NBC. I met him there in the newsroom when I first got a job as a production assistant."

"Not a copy girl?"

"No, I'd done that at my Dad's paper in Oakland. He was the Managing Editor of the Gazette. After college at Cal I went to New York, wanting to get into broadcast journalism." She smiled to herself. A long time ago, indeed.

"So you went with Tom Wells to Spain. For NBC?"

Meg nodded and took another sip of wine. "Tom was fearless—go anywhere for a story. NBC had two lines to Europe. American ITT owned the phone system in Spain—which worked much of the time. And the cable heads were in the Republican sector."

"And what about you—in Spain? Were you actually reporting, or were you just..."

Meg laughed. "Screwing? No. I was writing pieces about the Spanish women who were fighting—and other feature stories." A shadow crossed her face. "That time in Madrid is unforgettable. The Civil War was an unimaginable tragedy. Death surrounded us. It was a cruel, frustrating, horrifying fiasco. Franco's troops committed countless atrocities. As did the Communists and Anarchists—on a smaller scale. Life was cheap. And the governments of Britain, France and America looked the other way. What happened in Spain broke my heart."

2
Manhattan
October, 1936

When Tom and I stood on the deck of the Normandie as she slipped her moorings and slid away from the West 50th street dock on the Hudson, I could hardly keep from dancing in my new high-heeled red shoes. Instead, I waved wildly to our friends, my roommates and the boys from the newsroom who had come to see us off. Tugboats dragged the huge liner out into the river and then into the New York harbor and out to sea. The Nomandie was the most beautiful ship I had ever seen, and this was my first trip to Europe, and I was in love with Tom Wells, and I was on assignment to cover the civil war in Spain—well, sort of. I was Tom's production assistant for NBC radio. As we floated into the harbor I could see the WLW antenna poking up from our building in Rockefeller Center. 50 Rock we called it. I blew it a farewell kiss. When the tugboats cast off their lines, and the ship's vibration told us the engines had kicked in and the propellers were churning, I trembled with excitement. We were on our way to Spain. We were war correspondents.

As we entered the open sea the chill October wind set us shivering in our trench coats, and we scurried below to investigate our cabins. The art deco décor in tourist class was not as elegant as that of first class, but it seemed fantastically luxurious to me. Since coming to New York I had been sharing a basement apartment in the Village with three other girls, two violinists and a ballet dancer. The violinists played in a WPA orchestra, supported by Roosevelt's New Deal. The country was still mired in the Great Depression. People were desperate to find work, and panhandlers begged on the city's streets. The luxury of the Normandie was a shocking contrast, and I felt some guilt in feeling such pleasure. But I was a young and didn't dwell on it.

Tom and I had separate cabins, of course. We had become lovers two months earlier, but in the 30's nice girls like me didn't flaunt their affairs. We were circumspect. I remember feeling sophisticated and daring, thoroughly enjoying the thought that I had a bona fide lover. Tom had a Village apartment all his own. He was twenty-eight years old, an accomplished journalist with a shock of thick blond hair, six feet tall, whose dark blue eyes were filled with light. He had worked for NBC for three years. His specialty was European news, and when the Spanish generals began their rising, their insurgency, it was natural that he would be sent to cover the story.

Tom wangled my job for me, his blue-eyed, 24-yr old brunette assistant who spoke a fluent Spanish. Nobody in the newsroom was fooled and I was teased mercilessly, but I couldn't care less. Spain would be the adventure of my life, the beginning of my career—and I would be traveling alone with Tom Wells. I quickly began reading whatever I could lay my hands on about what was happening in Spain, the European and American response to the fascist insurgency and the German and Italian fascists' preparations for war. I also went shopping for new clothes.

The voyage to Le Havre took only four days. The wind was strong, but the weather remained fair. Although neither Tom nor I were a bit seasick, we spent a good part of the voyage in bed. I believe we both felt that we should grasp the moment, enjoy our youth before we faced the unknown dangers in Spain. After making love, we'd lazily exchange confidences, events in our lives we hadn't yet had the opportunity to talk about. In those few idle shipboard days we had time to spare. We smoked cigarettes, the ashtray propped on Tom's bare chest. I told him about my mother dying of flu in the 1918 epidemic. "I was only six and felt lost without her. Dad threw himself into his work, often taking me with him to the newsroom, but I really missed my mother. Fortunately, Dad hired a wonderful Mexican housekeeper, Caridad."

"And that's how you learned Spanish."

"Right. I can make good enchiladas, too."

He laughed and pushed a strand of my black hair from my eyes. "But Meg, I've been wondering how you got those blue, Irish eyes, the dark lashes. Your Dad isn't Irish with a name like Austin."

"My Mom's father was from Dublin. But enough about me. I know you went to Georgetown University and lived all over the world—with your diplomat father. But tell me more."

"You don't want to hear the list of countries, I'm sure. And the saga of a State Department brat is nothing I want to dwell on at this moment. I guess the important thing is that I'm fascinated by what's going on in the world, and I want to be where it's happening." As he spoke he seemed charged with energy, restless, inquisitive. His eyes were fixed on me as if I were the only person in the world who interested him. He kissed my neck. "But to tell you the truth, at this moment I like being right here in this bed."

Besides making love, we walked the lovely teak decks, of course, drank good Scotch whiskey, dined and danced. We even worked an hour or so. We each had brought portable typewriters and wrote about the incredible Normandie and the characters we met. Those four days of the voyage seemed like the happiest days of my life.

Our trip to Paris from Le Havre was smooth enough. We each had only one suitcase and a portable typewriter. I had puzzled over what to pack, not sure of what my life in Spain would consist of. Tom had warned me that Madrid could become cold and I had included a warm green pullover and carried a trench coat with pockets deep enough to hold my reporter's notebook. My suitcase was stuffed with clothes that were easy to care for except for one slinky ice-blue silk evening gown. For travel I wore a wool suit of black and white check, a black cashmere sweater—and, of course, my red high-heeled shoes and a jaunty red beret. I was ready for my great adventure.

I fell in love with Paris almost the moment we emerged from the railroad station. After we checked in with the NBC office we had time to wander on our own. Arm in arm we sauntered along the wide boulevards and narrow back streets near the Eglise St Germaine and our small hotel, the Dauphine. I loved the arched bridges over the glistening Seine and the old gray stone buildings with their lacy ironwork balconies. I couldn't see enough of the shop windows glowing with chic dresses, mouth-watering pastries, brilliant vegetables—and the Jeu de Paume with its Renoirs and Monets. And lovers everywhere! We strolled through the Jardin de Luxemburg, kicking the crunchy golden leaves that carpeted the ground, laughing, twirling with them as they rose into the air. I fell even more in love with Tom and didn't want to leave Paris. I couldn't imagine a more romantic city. Lovers embraced by the Seine and in the park and Tom and I felt free to copy them.

The sun shone, and although there was a slight chill in the air, our third day in Paris was warm enough to sit outside the Cafe de Flore on Blvd St Germaine sipping our tiny cups of coffee. Tom sprawled on his small wicker chair, his fedora pushed back on his thick blonde hair. I loved the way he spoke French so easily. He'd spent two years here as a boy attending a Lycée and knew his way around. To me he seemed incredibly sophisticated. With the sun shining on my face and the taste of coffee on my lips I tried to manufacture some reason to stay in Paris. "Tom," I said, "I would love to stay here a few more days. What do you think? Why don't we do a piece on the non-intervention policy. Interview a few diplomats. Do stories like Leon Blum, a Socialist, cutting off armaments to the Spanish Republic—or are the French bourgeois afraid of a Russian-type revolution? That sort of thing."

He shook his head. "It's been done. They're all scared of Bolshevism, of course. The Brits particularly." He fished a pack of Luckies from his shirt pocket and offered me one. I slid it from the pack and he leaned forward and lit my cigarette with his silver Ronson lighter, then his own. Squinting his eyes, he sighed. "It would be great to stay longer, but our assignment is Spain. We have reporters here in Paris who've been covering the Blum-Eden story. The other big story from Paris is Cominterns' International Brigade."

"Comintern?" I had heard the term and knew it had something to do with the Communist Party, but I wasn't sure.

"Comintern is short for the international Communist organization." He tapped the ash from his cigarette into the tin ashtray in the middle of the small table. "And I just checked with UPI. In two days 500 volunteers will be leaving from the Gare de Austerlitz to fight for the Republicans. If we don't get to the frontier before that, it will take ages to cross into Spain. There'll be a bottleneck. Border officials love to make a crossing complicated."

"Who are they, the volunteers, French leftists? Communists? Intellectuals?"

Tom frowned. "Some intellectuals. More than half are Communists. But mostly they're unemployed workers, idealistic union members, who want to fight fascism before it takes over all of Europe. Apparently, this first group is mostly French—but also Polish and German exiles—and an Englishman or two. They say hundreds of men have already found their way to Barcelona—Socialists, Trotskyists, Anarchists, exiles from fascist countries, Brits, a few Americans. We'll be able to get their story when we get to Spain." He leaned toward me and took hold of my hand. "I'd like to stay here, believe me, but you'll love Spain. At least I hope it isn't already in ruins, 'though with German planes Franco can do plenty of damage—even in only three months." His expression darkened. "We have a job to do, and I hope I haven't made a mistake persuading you to come with me." He reached toward me and touched my cheek.

I reassured him he hadn't made a mistake, I would be just fine and that it was the experience of a lifetime.

The next few days were exhausting. The Paris to Perpignon train was crowded with weary-looking men carrying paper-wrapped bundles and wearing work boots and workers' caps. We found space in one of the compartments and squeezed in between them. At first none of the men spoke. They seemed tense and furtive. After a few moments, one of them offered a cigarette to his companion—in English. We introduced ourselves, and after chatting a while, I felt certain the men were on their way to fight for Republican Spain. Obviously, Tom had come to the same conclusion. "We're journalists on our way to Barcelona and Madrid," he explained, smiling. "We'll be in the Republican sector. We're supposed to report the news without bias, but personally we're both strongly anti-fascist."

The men grinned, shifted in their seats and began to talk freely. They were British shipyard workers. They'd crossed the English Channel on the excursion ferry and didn't have papers for Spain. They'd have to hike over the Pyrenees when they arrived in Perpignon. "The Basque smugglers will guide us," the man sitting across from me said. "Then we'll go after those buggers, those fascist insurgent generals."

I found myself watching these men. They were edgy, unshaven and angry-eyed. They had a mission, and they were aching to fight. What would happen to them? I had read about the slaughter of Republican fighters by the Nationalists when they took over Badajoz near the Portuguese border. The Nationalists had driven whoever they thought had been fighting against them into the bullring and machine-gunned them in batches. 1,800 men and boys. Now, for the first time, with my eyes fastened on these men sitting across from me, I began to feel the bloody reality of the war. Hardly an adventure.

In Perpignon, near the Spanish border, we met a flushed-faced, hard-bitten journalist friend of Tom's who told us to remove our bourgeois clothing before we got to Barcelona. "The Anarchists rule the city, their red and black flags are all over the place. They harass anyone who looks at all rich," he said, grinning. "Wear old clothes. Look proletarian. The rampage of killings has pretty much stopped, though fascists, priests and nuns have either all been shot or fled the country."

I was shocked, of course. I hadn't believed the atrocity stories—at least not the ones on the Republican side, and I didn't know what Anarchist harassment would entail. Before we left Perpignon, I removed my red shoes and smart suit and exchanged them for tan tailored slacks, white blouse, green sweater and walking shoes—all new. Tom had brought dungarees, scuffed up shoes and a well-worn sweater. When Tom saw me he grinned and gave me a hug. "You don't quite make it, doll. You still look like a well-heeled California girl. Strictly bourgeois. We'll have to find you something old and patched."

"For Christ sake, Tom, how? Where?" The only thing I could think of to look proletarian was to remove my makeup and smear soot from the window ledge onto my slacks and shoes. Tom reached for my hands and drew me toward him. "Meg, don't worry. We have our journalist's papers. You'll be fine. I was just teasing."

Crossing the frontier from France to Spain was a nightmare of officialdom. Our passports were checked and re-checked, our journalist papers, stamped, examined, and stamped again. No Anarchists here, obviously, but as the train traveled closer to Barcelona, I began to see how poor people were. Women with baskets containing scrawny chickens or piles of wilted vegetables climbed on the train. They wore black dresses, rope-soled shoes, and black crocheted shawls covering their heads. Their faces were gaunt and sun-hardened.

When we entered Barcelona I noted the red and black flags fluttering from almost every building. Anarchists. My test would begin.

3
Barcelona
October, 1936

When we arrived in Barcelona high clouds blocked out the sun and a chill wind blew from the sea. The taxi we hailed to take us to the hotel was painted black and red like the Anarchist flags. "Salud, comaradas," the driver called out as we piled our luggage into the cab, not *buenas tardes* or *señores*, I noted. But to my relief, he didn't glare at me for looking like a bourgeois California girl. Our journalist informant had been correct, however, about the red and black flags. They flew from almost every building and the trams were also painted red and black.

The men walking along the crowded streets were dressed in blue overalls or faded corduroy with red scarves around their necks and workers' caps or black berets. I didn't see anyone in military uniform. Nor did I see anyone in suits or smart dresses. The women were almost all in black with black shawls over their shoulders. Had the wealthy disappeared, or did they dress like workers to remain unnoticed?

Tom was staring out the window, taking it all in. We didn't speak. As we drove along a wide avenue the driver told us was Las Ramblas, we could hear martial music blasting from speakers attached to the streetlights. The street was in poor repair, and the town looked somehow untidy with cluttered sidewalks and peeling paint. The gray sky didn't help. I noted a bakery shop where a long queue of weary-looking people waited to enter. We passed three burned and collapsed churches.

I thought about what we were told about the killings of priests, monks and nuns. I hadn't believed the stories at first, assuming they

13

were rightist propaganda, but when I saw the burned churches, I realized the stories were perhaps true. Why was the Catholic clergy so hated? Spanish workers had become anti-clerical, I knew, but killing nuns? I thought of the sisters who taught at the Catholic school Caridad had persuaded me to attend. They were strict and often mean and I begged my father to let me go to public school, which he did. The Church controlled education here in Spain. Was it possible that men killed nuns and priests not only because of the Church's ostentatious display of wealth and toadying to the rich, but because of smoldering resentments they'd harbored since childhood?

When we arrived at the hotel Tom paid the driver, adding a tip. The driver smiled and returned the change. He shook his finger. "No, no propina, comarada!" Astonished, Tom glanced at me and shrugged. He thanked the driver, who helped me with my suitcase. Tom carried his own, catching on to the egalitarian spirit.

I felt dazed. Somehow, here in Catalonia during the last three months a workers' revolution had occurred and I'd known nothing about it. Maybe I had been reading the wrong newspapers or listening to biased reporters. We stashed our luggage in my room and shut the door. Only then did we talk. "No wonder France and England are afraid of helping the Republic," I said. "This town has had a Bolshevik-style revolution."

Tom peered out the window. "It sure seems like it, but Anarchist, not Bolshevik. The workers' unions are powerful here in Barcelona, and the two Anarchist unions have a huge membership." He retrieved his notebook from his suitcase and shoved it into his shirt pocket. "When we passed the bar I saw two guys who look familiar. I think one of them is a reporter for a Chicago paper. Let's go down and find out what they know. I could use a drink, anyway."

"I'll join you in a few minutes. I need to clean up a little."

"OK. I'll see you downstairs. First, I'll put my stuff in my own room." He picked up his suitcase and typewriter, and laughing, gave me a quick kiss. "I don't want the boys to get the wrong idea."

When I entered the barroom combed and clean and wearing my dark green sweater and tan slacks, Tom waved to me from a corner table. Two other men were seated around it, plates of tapas and glasses of red wine cluttering its surface. They all rose as I approached, and stared at me as if I were some strange creature from an unknown world. "Sit down, please," I said laughing. "Just pretend I'm one of the boys."

"One of the boys! Out of the question," said one of the men who I guessed would be in his early thirties. He had brown hair, brown eyes, and wore a rumpled shirt under a zippered jacket. He gave me a charming smile. "It's like a breath of spring when a lovely young woman joins us old hacks."

Tom introduced me. Rumpled shirt was Ralph Fitzgerald of the *Chicago Tribune* and the other fairer, thinner, more tidily dressed journalist, was Anthony Thomas, of the *Manchester Guardian*.

Ralph peered at me closely through his horn-rimmed glasses. "Wells, here, says you're the daughter of Fred Austin of the *Oakland Gazette*."

"Yes, do you know him?"

"We met at the Press Club in San Francisco some years ago. A swell guy."

Tom called the waiter to bring more tapas and a glass of wine for me. Then after the initial exchange of small talk, they returned to the subject I assumed I had interrupted: the militias, the variety of organizations, and the extent of their cooperation. At first, their talk was like alphabet soup. I heard the letters UGT, CNT- FAI, POUM, PSUC. At a pause in the fast exchange of talk—journalists are always voluble—I begged the men to slow down. "I'm confused. I can't keep all those organizations straight. I know about the Socialists and I've seen the Anarchist flags all over the town, but did you say POUM? Who are they?"

Ralph nodded. He spoke slowly as if I were a child. "There are four major organizations. Besides the Socialists and the Anarchists, the other two are POUM, which is a Trotskyist Party, and the PSUC, the Communist Party."

Tom fished a cigarette from his shirt pocket and offered the pack around the table. "Thanks," said Ralph, "I'll take one, but you better hang on to your cigarettes. They're getting scarce." The waiter served me my wine and returned to the bar for the tapas.

Tom nodded. "Maybe I'll finally be forced to cut down. But to get back to what you were saying, the Communist Party here takes its orders from Stalin, right? And Stalin doesn't think much of Trotsky."

Ralph gave a grim smile. "So we've heard! As you know, Stalin's executing his rivals, his old Bolshevik buddies at the moment. And

Trotsky is a former Bolshevik, Lenin's heir apparent. Stalin and Trotsky are in a blood battle."

At this moment I was feeling incredibly ignorant and naïve. I had been so thrilled with the idea of the struggle between Socialist-Communist ideals and fascism that I hadn't read the fine print, so to speak. I had heard about the show trials in Moscow and knew that Stalin was a tough dictator, but I hadn't wanted to learn more. Hitler and Mussolini's fascism seemed so much more evil and dangerous. I turned to Ralph. "So are POUM members and Communists cooperating?"

"Surprisingly, here in Catalonia, at this point at least, all the organizations are cooperating—including POUM and the Communists. In spite of their differences."

Tom blew out a trail of smoke. "I wonder how long the cooperation will last?"

Anthony Thomas spooned some tapanada onto his small plate the waiter had just set on the table. "Who knows? I suspect not for long." He spoke with a slight Lancashire accent similar to that of my Grandfather Austin. "The Anarchist unions have organized workers' committees to run the factories and farm cooperatives in the country. It's remarkable, but Catalonia is actually a workers' and peasants' state."

I sipped my wine, trying to absorb what I was hearing. There really had been a revolution here. "What about the Communists in the government? Do they go along with what's happening here?"

"So far," Anthony answered, "but from what I hear they're far from happy about it. They get their orders from Stalin, who backs the democratic Republic, not revolution. At the moment, at least. Since the pact between Russia and France, Stalin wants to avoid frightening the Western democracies. The fight against fascism must come first."

Tom was eying the tapanada. "And what about the militias? I understand each group organizes its own."

"Right," Ralph said. "They're spread out up on the ridge that faces Nationalist-held Huesca, the front line. They're pitifully equipped. A few rifles, not much ammo, no artillery. No proper uniforms. Many of the militiamen don't know how to shoot. I was up there two days ago. The Anarchist troops don't have officers. They don't salute, and they almost have to vote before an action." He laughed. "But they're a brave lot, that's for sure."

I scooped some tapanada onto my plate. "But is it really true that the leftist atrocities have stopped here in Barcelona?" I was still picturing the burned churches and imagining the shooting of nuns.

Ralph gave me a reassuring smile. "So they say. It all happened in the first weeks after the insurgents' rising. The workers and peasants were incredibly poor, badly treated by some of their bosses and landowners, ignored and condescended to by the clergy. They went on a rampage. They exploded with the rage and resentments they'd been forced to suppress. It's also true that delinquent gangs did many of the shootings. The Anarchists had emptied the prisons."

"But the violence stopped."

"Right. A committee of control was formed. Also the Civil Guard remained with the Republicans. They helped stop the killings."

I felt myself relax. Maybe I needn't worry about what clothes I wore. A childish thought, I knew, but I'd been frightened by the Perpignan journalist.

"But the fascist violence continues," Anthony from Manchester said, spearing an olive from the tapa dish with his small fork. "When they take over a town they shoot anyone they believe was sympathetic to the Republic. Garcia Lorca, for instance. They maintain a rule of terror. Streams of refugees from the Nationalist regions flock here every day. We hear their stories of torture and murder. Thousands have been shot."

Before we could say more, the bartender tuned up the volume on the radio placed on the bar. I listened carefully. It was a news report from Madrid. The Spanish was somewhat difficult for me to understand, since I spoke Latin-American Spanish and didn't lisp the letter *s*. But I soon caught on. Tom gave me a questioning look. His Spanish was rudimentary. "The announcer's reporting that a delivery of airplanes and tanks will be arriving from Russia for the Republic, but Nationalist troops are close to Madrid and an attack is expected—and someone else will be reporting in a moment." Then a woman began speaking. She had a mellow, deep voice and spoke with some passion about the International Brigades that had been organized by the Comintern. The first contingent would be arriving at Alicante the next day, she said. She ended her report with a resounding *no pasarán!*, they shall not pass. I turned to Ralph Fitzgerald. "That woman has an incredible voice. Do you know who she is?"

"Dolores Ibarruri, better known as La Pasionaria. She's a Communist deputy from Asturias, a member of the government Cortes, the parliament. *No pasarán* has become her trademark since her first radio speech on the day of the uprising. She's an eloquent speaker and propaganda writer. Devout Communist. The people love her. I think she's taken the place of the Virgin Mary for these anti-church Spaniards. They worship the ground she walks on."

I wanted to get to know this woman. I could hardly wait to get to Madrid.

When we returned to my room after dinner Tom closed the door firmly and latched it. He put his hands on my shoulders and held me at arms' length. "Our first night in Spain," he said. "So how do you feel?" His deep blue eyes flickered in the lamplight.

"I'm not sure. It's not what I expected, but I'm excited."

"So what did you expect?"

"Soldiers marching, gunfire, guitars, flamenco dancers, sunlight. Coming into town I saw shabbily dressed people, but no uniforms and a cloudy sky. The music playing on the loudspeakers sounded like revolutionary songs—not flamenco."

Tom gave me a rueful smile. "You'll hear gunfire, I'm sure of that. We didn't see uniforms because, as Ralph told us, the militias are so poorly equipped."

I pulled away from him and sat on the bed. "So what are you going to say about Barcelona when you file your story."

He stuffed his hands in his trouser pockets. "Not much. The town is filled with refugees fleeing from Franco's persecution. Militias have been organized and are at the front fighting Nationalist insurgents. The different organizations are cooperating. The militiamen are ill-equipped and are in desperate need of armaments."

"So nothing about the revolution that has taken place, the workers' committees, the factories in workers' control, the peasant collectives?"

"No, I don't think so. It would be counterproductive. I think I'll downplay the revolutionary aspect of what's happened in Barcelona. To fight fascism the Republic needs guns, artillery, planes, tanks. France, Britain and the US must come to the rescue. American Catholics have been shocked enough by the atrocity stories, the killings of the clergy that the right-wingers have broadcast so repeatedly. The fight against fascism is what's important. Hitler is re-arming. We've got to stop fascism here!"

I didn't know how to respond. What he said was true—but... As reporters weren't we supposed to be objective? I locked eyes with him. "What about the reporter's holy grail—objectivity?"

"It's just not possible. You have to take sides. There's no way you can stay impartial." He flopped down beside me and pulled me toward him on the bed. "Lets' change the subject, for Christ's sake. We're in Spain. Beautiful, tragic, dramatic Spain. How can anyone be objective?" He kissed me hard and we began to make love.

4
Madrid
November, 1936

When we arrived in Madrid and checked in with the Ministry of Information, we were billeted at the elegant art nouveau Hotel Florida, along with other reporters known to be sympathetic to the Republic. I was stunned when I eyed the soaring ten story space above the atrium in the center of the hotel. On each floor rooms opened onto an open balcony-like corridor overlooking the atrium. The balcony railings were of black wrought iron in a lacy design. On the atrium floor was a cluster of tables and chairs, which when we arrived were all occupied. The place buzzed with energy. Journalists, almost all male, were arguing, talking, laughing—and drinking. A well-stocked bar stood at the side. Our rooms were on the third level. Mine even had a bathroom with a marble floor. There were only a few women to be seen, and from the way they were dressed I suspected that some of these were prostitutes. The hotel stood on the Plaza Callao on the Gran Via in the center of Madrid.

We all knew that Madrid would soon become a target of Franco's Nationalist troops. We already heard the thud of artillery shells as they exploded at the edge of the city. The big guns were placed west of town, across the river Manzanares. I experienced my first air raid about a week after Tom and I arrived in Madrid. Tom was telephoning his story to the NBC news bureau in Paris from the Telefonica building across the street from our hotel. We were on the tenth floor of the thirteen-story cement and steel building when a siren began to wail. Through the window of the glass booth Tom gestured wildly for me to get downstairs. Then I heard what sounded like a bomb exploding in the distance.

I ran toward the elevator, but fearing an electricity shut-down, took the stairs. I raced down the ten flights, the heels of my red shoes clattering on the steps. As I descended, the noise from outside the building was deafening: alarms sounded, church bells rang, airplane engines roared and explosions boomed. When I reached the ground floor I leaned back against an inside wall, breathing hard. Should I try to find the stairs to the basement? The lobby was empty except for a guard who huddled against the wall opposite the main door. I pressed my hands tightly over my ears. A loud explosion nearby shook the floor of our building, which felt rather like the earthquakes I'd experienced in California. My teeth chattered and I felt an inner confusion, a kind of disbelief. This was an air-raid. I could die.

A woman dressed in black dashed inside the building seeking shelter. When she spoke to the guard I recognized her resonating voice. It was Dolores Ibarruri, La Pasionaria, I was certain. She moved rapidly but regally to one of the marble benches that were placed along the inner wall by the elevator. Self-controlled and calm, sitting with straight back, she cocked her head to one side, as if she were listening to the direction the planes were flying and where the bombs were falling. She was not beautiful, but had a striking face, a strong profile, aquiline nose, wide mouth and fierce black eyes. Her shining dark hair was pulled back into a loose bun.

I continued to shiver with fright as I listened to the drone of airplanes and the bomb blasts. Tom had told me the best way to overcome fear during artillery or air attacks was to think about the story you could write. I watched La Pasionaria and decided to take advantage of this frightening moment to introduce myself to her. I left the spot against the wall where I had been huddling and scurried toward her bench.

"Excuse me, Señora Ibarruri," I said, holding my trembling arms close to my chest, yelling to be heard over the sound of the tumult overhead. I spoke in my Latin-American-accented Spanish, having given up trying to speak Castilian like the local Spaniards. "I've been wanting to meet you since I heard you speak on the radio. Me llamo Margarita Austin, una periodista de radio NBC." My voice quavered as I spoke.

21

"Mucho gusto," she answered in her mellifluous voice. We continued to converse in Spanish. "And you are from the United States? You are very young to be a reporter." She beckoned for me to sit beside her, then turned her head to listen to the planes. "Don't be frightened. The fascist generals announced yesterday that they would not bomb the Salamanca district because of the foreign embassies—just a few blocks away. They're concentrating on the workers' neighborhoods." She gave a grim laugh. "And the fascists say they expect to drink coffee on the Gran Via next week. They will need to think again." She stopped again to listen. The drone of the bombers was fading. "I think they're returning to their base. The Soviet fighters, the little Chatos, have chased them away. You will recognize the Chatos when you see them. They're a stubby biplane marked with a red band. "

I listened, hearing only the sound of ambulances or fire trucks. "Thank God they've gone," I murmured.

She gave me an odd look. "It's the Soviet planes and guns you should thank, and their brave pilots, not God."

I bit my lip, at a loss as to how to answer. I knew that now was my chance to ask her questions, to request an interview. I had to get my wits together. "Señora Ibarruri, you…" I took a deep breath.

"Please. Call me Dolores." She smiled. "Or Comrade."

I returned her smile, dug out my reporter's notebook from my bag. "OK, Dolores, you're a Cortes deputy, correct?"

"Claro. A Communist Party deputy to the parliament from Asturias."

"I have heard that Prime Minister, Largo Caballero has persuaded members of the Anarchist parties to join his government, and he's appointed four of these people to be on his cabinet. Do you approve?" I uncapped my green fountain pen, hoping for an answer. My hands had stopped shaking.

She sighed and stood, as if ready to leave. "I hope we can all work together to defeat our perfidious enemies. If the Anarchists are willing to discipline themselves, to stop insisting on their goal of immediate revolution, and pour their energies into fighting Fascism on the side of democratic government, then I will do my best to work with them. But now I must get back to work. The bombing has stopped."

From the precision of her reply, I assumed she had answered this question before, possibly several times and was accustomed to being interviewed. "Dolores," I said quickly, "I would like to see you again. Your work is so important. I would like to interview you in depth. The American people need to hear the truth about what's happening here."

"I'm incredibly busy, but you're right. We need to change America's attitudes. American oil companies continue to send airplane and tank fuel to the fascists. The Church's propaganda has described us *Reds* as villainous devils, and Americans are afraid." She reached out to shake my hand. "I'll arrange something. Perhaps you can go with me on one of my tasks. I'll contact you. Where are you staying?"

"At the Florida, on the Plaza Callao, here on the Gran Via."

She laughed. "With all the other journalists. At least you speak Spanish, unlike most of your colleagues." She waved and strode out the door, nodding to the guard who gave her a worshipful look. For a moment I thought he was going to make the sign of the cross.

After La Pasionaria's regal exit, the elevator doors opened and Tom and Ralph Fitzgerald hurried toward me. We had traveled with Ralph and Anthony Thomas to Madrid in a hired car. "You're OK", Tom asked, giving me a tight hug.

I nodded. "And did you get your story filed?"

"Yes, in spite of the air-raid. I kept expecting the phone lines to go down or the electricity to be shut off."

"Telefonica is owned by American ITT," Ralph said. "They've done a good job of protecting the phone and cable lines. If the electricity shuts off their generator takes over. We all file our stories here from the press room. So far no problem—as long as a bomb doesn't hit the building. And it's made of concrete and steel, so it might be able to take hits."

"La Pasionaria was just here," I said, "She told me the fascist generals announced that the Salamanca district wouldn't be bombed. They expect to be drinking coffee on the Gran Via by the end of the week."

Ralph snorted. "I'll be damned. I guess they don't want to wipe out the classy neighborhoods. Lucky for us, anyway."

Tom took my arm as we walked toward the door. "Pasionaria was here!"

"Yes, she came inside for shelter. I asked her for an interview and she agreed!"

Tom gave my arm a congratulatory squeeze. "Good luck. An interview with her would make a great story."

We approached the door to the building, cautiously stepped outside and peered around us. There had been no damage on this section of the street, but a dark layer of smoke clung to the rooftops above us. I could hear the sirens of police cars or ambulances.

Ralph sniffed the air. "You can smell the burned buildings and gunpowder. From the tenth floor we saw fires in the suburbs. Hitler's Junkers were dropping incendiary bombs. And did you hear the siren warning us of an air-raid?"

I nodded.

"In the press room they told me it was mounted on a soldier's motorcycle. The guy zipped through the city streets from one neighborhood to another. Soldiers have been attaching sirens to the lamp posts for the next raid."

I shivered, the memory of the sound of bombs exploding in my ears. As we crossed the Gran Via on the way to our hotel, a truck flying a red flag passed slowly by. It was jammed with armed, khaki-uniformed men. On the roof of the cab a loudspeaker was exhorting the people of Madrid to fight their fascist enemies. "You must take precautions immediately. Franco's insurgent generals are planning a new attack. It must be repelled! Madrid is no longer the open and free city of yesterday. Today it is a besieged fortress."

Men and women on the sidewalk stopped to listen. Their tense faces expressed a combination of fear and determination. My own gut had tightened. "A besieged fortress," I repeated.

Tom's eyes followed the truck as it went by. "It's Communist Party rhetoric, but it looks as though Madrid is Franco's next target."

I watched the truck move slowly down the street. I noted the red flag, the rifles and the khaki uniforms. "Are they part of the Communist Party 5th Regiment you told us about, Ralph?"

He nodded. "They've taken a big role in organizing the defense of Madrid. They work closely with that Russian, General Goriev."

I was now truly in a war zone. I glanced at Tom—then Ralph. They didn't look scared. Excited, maybe. Stimulated. Ready to be tested in battle. What would Tom think of me if he knew how afraid I was, how uncertain I was feeling about doing a journalist's job in the midst of bombs and gunfire—and death?

As we walked toward the hotel, another truck passed carrying men and women holding picks and shovels. "They're finally digging trenches and stringing barbed wire," Tom said grimly. He turned to me. "The government has been against digging trenches. They've been stuck in the Middle Ages, thinking they can still fight face-to-face with the visor up, like don Quixote. They've considered cowering in a ditch dishonorable. The militias think otherwise. They've experienced air attacks."

For a moment I allowed myself to imagine being out in the open with bombs dropping around me and nowhere to hide. What a nightmare. Then another truck rode down the Gran Via flying the government flag. From a loudspeaker mounted on the truck's roof a voice announced, "all children, the sick and elderly will be evacuated to the coast at Levante. Parents, proceed with your children and elderly to the Atocha station as soon as possible."

I listened to the announcement with a sinking heart. "They're sending the children away. They're evacuating the city!"

Tom gave me a sympathetic look. "It's better not to have to worry about them. It's a scary thought, I know, but we'll be OK. We just have to be cautious and stay out of the firing line."

I stared at him, not knowing how to respond.

Later that evening when Tom and I were in the cellar restaurant of the Gran Via Hotel, where the Ministry of Information had arranged for the extranjeros de la prensa to dine together, a crowd of journalists came charging into the room. They clambered onto the plain wooden benches at the long plank tables and began shoveling down the food the servers put before them. The reporter from Manchester, Anthony Thomas, took his place on the other side of me. As he dug into his lamb stew, he told us he'd just come from the press briefing at the Junta de Defensa. "Lots of news tonight. You should have been there."

"I was calling in my story," Tom said, "and staying out of the way of the bombs. So tell us!"

"Franco's troops are massing west of the city—across the river by the open areas of Casa de Campo, the old royal hunting grounds. Their artillery is already in place. They have four attack columns that will attempt to cross the river. The assault is expected to begin tomorrow.

They're using the colonial troops under the command of Varela—Moroccans and Legionnaires." Anthony paused in his report to take a bite of his stew. I had heard of the Moroccans and the Foreign Legion. I certainly didn't want to be here in Madrid if *they* took the city. They had a reputation for rape and murder.

Tom frowned. "And what about the militias, the Brigades? Are they manning the line?"

"The Mixed Militias will move to the line tonight. The trade unions have organized their men: barbers, tailors, metal workers—even schoolteachers. Apparently, a battalion of women will guard the Segovia Bridge. They're already building more barricades and digging trenches."

"Do the militias have enough weapons?" I asked.

"Rifles, but damned little ammunition. And most have never even fired a rifle. It will be a miracle if the assault is stopped."

I glanced at Tom, curious about his reaction to the possibility of Franco's success. He looked perturbed, but still alert and excited.

Anthony continued. "The officer at the briefing also told us that reinforcements from Germany began to arrive in Seville for Franco's Nationalists three days ago. Bombers and fighters, called the Condor Legion, flown by Goering's Luftwaffe pilots. Each of four squadrons have twelve Junker 52 bombers. Also, Heinkel 51 fighters, anti-aircraft artillery, two tank squadrons and over 3,000 men."

I suddenly lost my appetite. My stomach had knotted.

"There's more." Anthony said. "The government is moving to Valencia tonight—at this moment. Largo Caballero made the announcement this afternoon. Lorries are already being loaded up with government files. The embassies will go too. The Junta de Defensa will rule the capital during the government's absence. General Miaja and the Russian, General Goriev, will work together. Colonel Voronov will be in control of the Russian artillery, although I hear few batteries have shells. All hell's going to break loose at dawn tomorrow."

My courage would now really be tested. I looked at Tom. His eyes were sparking with excitement and his cheeks had flushed. "I've got to get out there. See what's going on." He extricated himself from the bench. "Meg, I'll walk you to the hotel."

"Shouldn't I go with you? You might need Spanish." I tried to keep my voice steady as I spoke,

"No, Meg. It wouldn't be safe for you. I know some Spanish and plenty of French and German speakers are out there."

I hesitated, wanting to object, but at the same time I was relieved he didn't need my help. I was scared. I could hardly believe the war was on our doorstep—a mile or so away. It was really happening. Somehow I needed time to adjust to reality. "Franco could win!" I said, in disbelief.

"Well, one thing's for sure," Tom answered in a defiant tone. "The people of Madrid will give him a tough hard fight."

Anthony sighed. "And so many will die."

At the door of the Florida, as Tom walked off into the turmoil of trucks and horse-drawn wagons filled with refugees, women carrying babies and bundles, I almost called for him to stop. If I wanted to be a foreign correspondent, a tough journalist, I should be out there with him, or talking to those people out on the street, but I couldn't get myself to speak. Instead, in a daze, I turned into the Florida and headed for my room. Was I in shock? What had I expected? A romance? An adventure? I glanced down at my red shoes, which suddenly seemed ridiculous, and kicked them off. The floor was cold. I snatched the shoes from the floor and carried them to my suitcase stored in the carved oak armario. With a quick motion, I shoved them into the bottom of the bag, then reached for my sturdy brogues and tied them firmly.

5
Madrid
November 8, 1936

A glimpse of gray light edging the window curtain propelled me out of bed. Dawn was approaching. I knew that German Junkers would soon be droning overhead. Tom was curled up under the blanket sleeping soundly. I let him sleep, knowing he would be awakened soon enough. He had returned from the front in the early hours of the morning and had fallen asleep still in his clothes. Now I quickly used the bathroom and then threw on my warmest clothes: slacks, thick green sweater, wool socks and my brogues. It was cold and the hotel was unheated.

Lifting a corner of the curtain, I peered down onto the street three floors below. It was still dark, but I could see people, mostly women and children, moving rapidly along the sidewalks. The streetlights, which had been painted blue to make them less visible in air-raids, had not yet been turned off. Trucks and wagons rattled by, headed southeast, toward the Valencia highway or the Atocha train station, a few blocks away. The militias would already be in place in trenches around the western rim of the city on this side of the river, where Franco's Nationalist troops, on the opposite side, were poised for attack. From the tenth floor of Telefonica Tom had seen the big guns in place on the other side of the Manzanares. He had said that if my hotel room were on the west side of the hotel instead of the east it would be possible to see the artillery flashes from across the river when the assault began. It would also be more dangerous, since shells could hit the building from that close a distance, only a mile away.

Last night I had pulled myself together and done some work. Now I needed to get out on the street, observe, talk to people. Maybe I'd write about the evacuation of women and children from Madrid. The train station would be a good place to start. First, I had to talk to Tom in case he needed my help or could use the evacuation story in his broadcast. I was being paid by NBC to be his assistant, after all.

Suddenly, the air-raid siren began to shriek. It seemed to be coming from the light pole outside the hotel. I caught my breath. I began to shiver. Tom sat up in bed and groggily pushed aside the blanket. We both looked up at the ceiling, as if we were waiting for the sound of the bombers. Tom reached for his shoes. "We'd better get downstairs. Pronto!"

I snatched my coat from the chair where I'd left it the night before and shoved my notebook, small purse and two rolls of film into my pockets. Trying to keep from panic, I fished the Leica Dad had given me out of my bag and hung it around my neck. Tom dashed into the bathroom and I opened the windows as we had been instructed to do in an air-raid. Tom grabbed his jacket and notebook and we fled out the door and down the three flights of stairs.

Other half-dressed, unkempt hotel residents joined us, all heading for the cellar, where a bar had been set up. As we ran across the atrium we could hear the first wave of bombers flying overhead. Then came the sound of exploding bombs and rattling windows. The building shuddered. We raced down the steps to the cellar.

The hotel staff had set out a tray of bread rolls and coffee. They'd brought tables and chairs from the upstairs breakfast bar and were busily working at their tasks as if air-raids were a daily event. I admired their bravery. How did they do it! We found a spot at a corner table and hung on to our cups to prevent the coffee from spilling when the bombs exploded. The overhead lights swung from side to side and dishes rattled on the bar. I was scared, but less terrified than I'd been the day before. Could you get used to this? I looked at Tom, who seemed to be listening to the direction of the planes. Hardly anyone spoke. Two other men sat at the table, huddled over their coffee cups. Everyone seemed to be holding his breath, waiting—for what? The planes to fly away, a bomb to hit?

Eventually, the sound of the planes grew distant and the explosions stopped. Tom stood up. "They've gone, but they'll be back again when they re-load. They've taken over the airport at Getafe, just a few miles out of town. I need to run across the street to Telefonica. File my story about the Government move to Valencia while I can. The artillery will start soon." He moved toward the door.

I followed him. "Tom, do you need my help? Because if you don't I want to go to the Atocha station to check on the evacuation of women and children. Maybe shoot a few pictures." I forced my voice to remain steady. I was determined to be brave, to prove myself, to overcome my fear.

"Oh? The train station? Do you want to wait for me? I could go with you. I'll just be a half hour or so."

"I think I should get there as soon as possible—before the planes come back. Tom, I'll be fine." I straightened my shoulders. "I could meet you there if you like."

"Well, OK. I'll get there as soon as I can. But for Christ sake be careful. The subway stations are being used as air-raid shelters. You can duck down there if it gets rough." He put his arm around me as we went out into the gray light of dawn. He kissed me lightly. "Take care, doll! I'm not sure you should go off on your own like this—so soon."

"It's my baptism of fire. I have to do it, Tom. And I will be careful."

I watched as Tom dodged the traffic as he crossed the jammed Gran Via. The sky was growing lighter, the last of the stars had faded away and it was cold. I cinched the belt of my trench coat tightly around my waist, tucking my camera inside the collar. I headed up the street toward the train station, hurrying along with the crowd of fleeing women, children and the elderly. Trucks filled with armed men rolled by, going west toward the front. A pickup flying the red flag of the Communist Fifth Regiment drove by. At one of the plazas I spied a large sign. In big black letters it said, "IN BADAJOZ THE FASCISTS SHOT 2,000. IF MADRID FALLS THEY WILL SHOOT HALF THE CITY." I tugged my Leica out from under my coat and snapped a picture of the sign.

I'd walked two blocks before I heard the first deep thuds which I identified as artillery fire. The sound was coming from across the river and was different than the bomb explosions I'd heard the day before. A woman carrying a baby walking next to me cried out and began to run. Children sobbed in fright as their frantic mothers pulled them along the narrow street. I quickened my pace to a running walk, determined not to panic, fixing my eyes on the western side of the street, watching the smoke and dust rise up in the air as the firing continued, not knowing if we were in danger of falling shrapnel, or how far the cannons could fire. The smell of the gunpowder reminded me suddenly of the firecrackers I lit as a child on 4th of July. Some of the deep thudding-sounds seemed to be closer, but the explosions were farther away. I wondered if they were the Russian artillery. Maybe they'd found ammunition. I cut down one of the narrow passages that would lead to Paseo de Prado and the Atocha station, feeling somehow safer when I couldn't see the smoke rise. The firing continued. Women with frightened eyes ran by, babies in their arms.

When I reached the Prado, hearing planes above, I stopped. Looking up, I realized the planes were the Russian bi-plane fighters, the Chatos, flying in a V formation. Red bands encircled their dark green fuselages, just as La Pasionaria had described. Another formation of planes appeared from the west—bombers and their Fiat fighter escort. Nationalist planes. Italian. Tom had pointed them out to me two days before. Almost immediately, the Chatos broke formation, scattered and attacked the Fiats. I leaned against a building for a few seconds and watched in fascination as the planes swooped and rolled, their engines whining. Was this really happening? Planes right over my head? Russian planes shooting at Italian planes over a Spanish city? Insane! The people who had been running down the street also stopped for a moment to watch. When one of the Fiats turned back, a trail of black smoke streaming from its tail, the women and old men around me cheered. We then all hurried onward. The Junkers were dropping their bombs south of the city.

I entered the noisy, cavernous Atocha station and stepped into a crowd of white-faced adults and crying children huddled on the platform of track number eight. The sign above the platform said Valencia. The noise of the bombing and shelling continued and frantic mothers hugged their weeping children close. Sounds of voices and tramping feet and wheeled carriages echoed from the high curving glass ceiling of the station. Everyone carried large bundles or suitcases, and a few held dogs on leashes or cats in carrier bags. The dogs barked and the cats meowed plaintively. One child held a birdcage covered in a blue cloth. The children all had their names pinned to their coats.

I stopped to talk to a distraught woman holding a bundled-up newborn baby in her arms. A small girl, perhaps three years old, clung to the skirt of her coat. Two cardboard suitcases sat on the cement floor at the woman's feet. "Are you going with the evacuees to Valencia?" I asked, raising my voice to be heard above the clamor."

The woman nodded, her brow creased in a frown.

"The children will be safer there," I said.

"Yes, the bombs are so frightening. My husband insisted we evacuate Madrid. He's at the front. Defending the city with the other teachers at his school. I don't want to leave, but with the baby…"

At that moment, a train chugged into its place by the platform, its steam hissing noisily. The crowd surged forward. A woman dressed in black climbed onto the steps of one of the cars and held up her arm for attention. It was La Pasionaria. On the platform below her were two armed soldiers with red shoulder patches marked with the number five. I assumed they belonged to the Communist 5th Regiment. The crowd quieted immediately. Even the crying children lifted their tear-streaked faces as Pasionaria began to speak.

"This train will depart in twenty minutes and will take you to Levante, on the coast near Valencia." Her voice was resonant and strong. "You will be safe there. The good people of Levante have agreed to shelter you. Young women of the Communist Youth Organization will be your escorts. Soldiers of the 5th Regiment will insure your safety. In the meantime, those brave men and women remaining in Madrid will fight our perfidious enemies, the fascist insurgents, until they are beaten. So fear not. You will return to a free Madrid."

Flanked by the two guards, she stepped down from the platform and maneuvered through the crowd toward the entrance. As she passed within a few feet of me, I called to her, waving frantically. "Dolores," I cried, raising my voice over the noise of the crowd and the bombardment, "I've been hoping to see you."

Her guards shot me sharp looks, but Pasionaria eyed me with her raptor eyes and paused. "Ah yes. It's the American girl. The journalist."

"When can we meet?"

"Not now. I'm going to the front. When we push the fascists back. Then we can talk." She moved forward, but called out, "check at Gaylords. I'm sometimes there. Possibly this evening." She disappeared into the jumble of people and bundles, but I heard someone calling my name. I scanned the crowd. It was Tom.

"Good I found you!" Tom hugged me hard. "Was that La Pasionaria I just saw?"

"Yes. I asked her when I could see her, but she's going to the front. She said to check at Gaylords. Do you know what she means?"

"Hotel Gaylord isn't far from here. All the Russians stay there."

"Maybe I'll go there tonight—if they're still here! Have you heard anything? Is the line holding?"

"So they say. I wanted to find you first, see if you're OK, but I want to get out there."

"Actually, so do I Tom." My voice was unsteady. I took a deep breath to try to control my breathing.

"You want to go to the front?" Tom was giving me a perplexed look.

"Yes, Ralph said there's a battalion of women guarding the Segovia Bridge, remember? It would make a good story."

Tom fixed his eyes on me. "Are you up to it?"

I met his look. I was thinking of the movies I'd seen of the war in France: barbed wire, mud, trenches. "I'm not sure, but I want to try."

We had almost reached the door to the station. The crowd had diminished and the train was moving down the track. Mothers waved, tears flowing down their cheeks. I felt my own eyes begin to well up and then remembered my camera and that I was a journalist. I quickly brought my Leica to my eye and got shots of women with tear-drenched cheeks waving their soggy handkerchiefs. I tucked my camera back under my coat, and Tom and I emerged onto the street. Tom took hold of my arm and gave me an approving glance.

We hurried back to the Gran Via, hoping we could find a taxi to take us to the Segovia Bridge, which was on the front line. Tom could find out from there where the action was. His mood was electric. I wasn't sure if the possibility of a good story was what excited him, or the war itself. I was cold with fear, but was determined to stay in control. The bombers had disappeared, but the deep booming noises of the artillery had accelerated. The air was filled with the acrid smell of gunpowder.

We were crossing the Gran Via when we heard singing and a steady thumping sound that differed from that of the artillery. It was the beat of marching feet. We stopped to listen. "They're singing the *Internationale*," Tom cried. "It must be the International Brigades. They finally got here."

Thank God, I thought. Then I remembered what Pasionaria had said to me yesterday during the air-raid. Thank the Soviets for coming to the aid of Spain with their guns and tanks and all these brave volunteers from many countries, not God. But what was happening to my objectivity? I thought of Hitler's persecution of Jews, the Nuremberg Laws, the book burnings and censorship. It was impossible to be objective. I hated Hitler and fascists like him. Franco must not win. I was taking sides and I knew it.

We stood on the edge of the broad sidewalk and watched the men march by. The soldiers marched smartly, dressed in khaki uniforms with metal helmets. The first group was singing the *Internationale* in German. They were German and Austrian exiles, of course—Nazi-persecuted Communists or Jews. Other Brigades followed singing in French, English, Italian and other languages I didn't recognize—perhaps Polish or Hungarian. It was a moving sight. I felt myself caught up in the drama and emotion of the moment. The song was so rousing, and the men had come from all over the world to fight fascism and save the Spanish people and perhaps Europe—from tyranny.

I was a Roosevelt Democrat, not a Communist, but I believed in liberty and justice for the *workers of the world*, and the marching men singing with such passion brought tears to my eyes. *Arise ye prisoners of starvation* were the only words to the song I knew, which now I'd heard in several languages. Above us, Madrileños emerged from their apartments where they had been hiding from the bombs and leaned over their lacy wrought-iron balconies. They waved handkerchiefs and Republican flags and called out "Viva la Republica, viva los Rusos."

"People must think they're all Russians," Tom said.

I looked up at the emotion-choked Spaniards. "They're probably thinking about those Soviet fighters they saw chasing away the Italian fighters and scaring off the Junkers this morning. Or maybe they know the Brigades were organized by the Comintern."

"They know that Russia is the only country willing to fight the fascists. Communists against fascists. Where are the Western democracies?"

The Brigade disappeared down the Gran Via, and we continued on our way to the river. Tom boosted me onto the back of a Citroen truck stopped in traffic then hoisted himself next to me. It was headed for the front. We would find our way to the Segovia Bridge from there. We stood clinging with both hands to the truck's high railing as it zigzagged around mule-drawn wagons, bicycles, taxis and stalled automobiles. The truck bed was crowded with men standing shoulder to shoulder carrying rifles. They were not in uniform, but wore corduroy trousers, worn zippered jackets and peaked caps. They smelled of sweat and musty woolens. The men gave me a perfunctory glance and then continued to focus their eyes sharply on the street ahead of us. They didn't speak. The man next to me stood with his chin out and his shoulders back in a determined stance. His eyes were dark and fierce, but flickered with what I believed must be fear.

The sun was shining, but my hands were stiff with cold as I clutched the icy metal railing. The sound of the artillery grew louder as we approached the river. At each boom of the big guns, my heart lurched. The truck stopped at a barricade of stones, rubble and rolled up mattresses guarded by two men who were crouched behind it, their rifles propped in a niche in the barricade. Almost before the driver had put on his brakes, the men riding with us jumped off the truck, and bending over, their heads down, rushed down the street toward the noise of the firing.

Tom and I were the last to climb down onto the pavement. We hopped over the scattered debris, the pieces of brick, masonry and glass and crouched in an open doorway of a damaged brick building. Tom pulled a map from his pocket and we both studied it. Tom pointed to a spot on the map. "We're just past the North Railroad Station, here." He tapped the map again. "General Varela's Nationalist artillery is here, on the other side of the river. His Moroccan troops are coming through the old royal hunting grounds, the Casa del Campo. They'll try to cross the river to capture Madrid." He moved his finger down the map. "The

Segovia Bridge is here, only two blocks south of us, which is one of the ways they could get across, although they seem to be targeting the San Fernando Bridge, a little north of here." He touched the map again. "We could take this street parallel to the river on the other side of the Royal Palace. It has high walls. I noticed it from Telefonica. We'd be a couple of blocks from the front and have some protection from the shelling."

My breathing was ragged, but I had scrutinized the map as he spoke, and I wanted to get on with it. "OK. Let's go." We locked eyes. Tom put the map back in his pocket and took hold of my hand. "You're sure you want to do this."

I nodded and began to move forward. We hugged the walls as we hurried along the debris-strewn street. The sound of the artillery became somewhat fainter as we moved the two blocks south. At the corner two armed women emerged from sandbagged bunkers and stopped us. They questioned us sternly. We showed them our Journalist's ID, and I explained why we were here.

They returned our ID's and we continued toward the river. The street that led to the bridge was barricaded with stones, sandbags and debris. On both sides of the bridge trenches had been dug in the grass of the park-like approach to the river. Piles of rocks and sandbags stretched along their tops of the trenches. We could see rifles protruding, but the women soldiers were keeping under cover. The river was only about fifty feet wide. I hadn't realized how narrow it was.

A guard watched our approach and pointed a rifle at us. "What is your business here?" she shouted. She couldn't be more than eighteen and although she held herself erect and her expression was stern, I couldn't help but see that she was a very pretty girl with round black eyes and dark curly hair under her khaki forage cap.

"We explained again who we were and showed our papers.

"Pués, what do you want to see?" She jumped back into the trench and beckoned us to follow her. She was wearing a uniform of khaki overalls over her slender but curvaceous form. We squatted next to her on the rocky floor of the trench. Four other young women soldiers were crouched, kneeling on one knee, their rifles aimed toward the other side of the river. The trench smelled of damp earth, newly dug. Water puddled in between the river stones that made up the floor of the ditch.

I pulled out my camera and asked the guard if I could take her picture. She shook her head and glared at me. "No!"

I realized my mistake, feeling like an idiot, a greenhorn. She wouldn't want to be associated with the fighting if Franco won. She would be shot immediately. I tucked the camera away and asked if she would answer a few questions. She was unenthusiastic, but didn't turn away.

"We've been told this group is a trained battalion of women. How long have you been in training and are you members of any particular organization?"

"The Communist Party, of course." she said quickly. "And we've been training since the fascist uprising in July. But, really, this is not a time to answer questions. We must keep a sharp lookout on the opposite side of the bridge. If necessary we will blow it up. By no means will any of those Moroccan butchers cross the Segovia Bridge." Her eyes narrowed and her mouth tensed. I had heard of the ferocious African army, the dreaded Moors. They had a reputation for rape and of being quick with their knives.

Tom was peering over the edge of the trench. "Ask her if they have explosives here?"

I repeated Tom's question in Spanish.

"Yes, in that trench below—next to the bridge supports—are two Asturian miners. Men with dynamite. They know what to do. But now you should leave. You have no business here. Go!"

I thanked her and Tom wished her luck, "mucha suerte!" Tom had picked up a few useful phrases in Spanish. We climbed out of the trench and retraced our steps at a running walk. When we reached the wall separating us from the river, Tom stopped. "Meg, now I need to get closer to the fighting, and I don't think you should come with me."

I hesitated. Was I ready to witness trench warfare? I could hear the sharp explosions of artillery fire and the rattle of machine guns as we drew closer to the center of the attack. And is this what I wanted to write about? What I found compelling was the war's heartbreaking effect on the population, especially its women and children. I was anxious to get back to the hotel to write up what I'd seen and heard. At the same time, I wanted to be one of the boys. "Tom, if the women of Madrid can be at the front so can I, but to tell you the truth, I'd really like to get back to the hotel and write about the train station and Pasionaria. And it's not because I'm afraid. Although I *am* afraid—but I really want to write about what's happening to the people here."

He gave me an appraising look, as if measuring the extent of my fear. "OK. But let's find you a ride."

We walked quickly to the corner where we had jumped off the truck. Another truck, a big Renault, was just unloading a group of armed men. Tom asked the driver to give me a ride back into town, and the harried man thrust open the cab door. "Señorita, let's get you out of here!"

"Be careful, Tom," I called as I pulled myself up into the truck.

Tom slammed the door closed. "Don't worry, I will. See you back at the hotel!"

The driver shifted gears and the truck lurched forward, bumping over the rubble. He let me off at the Gran Via and I ran along the pavement to the Florida. Although the shelling continued, the bombers had not returned to the town center, and since my room was on the side of the hotel facing away from the front line, I was out of the line of fire.

Peeling off my coat and removing my Leica from around my neck, I sat at my typewriter. I slid a cigarette from the pack of Luckies next to me, lit it with a flimsy wooden match from a tiny box, and smoked a while, calming myself, marshaling my thoughts. I stubbed out the cigarette and began. I wrote about the evacuation of children, Pasionaria's speech, the International Brigade, and the battalion of women at the Segovia Bridge. It was too much to deal with, and the words didn't flow. I lit another cigarette. As I breathed smoke into my lungs, I thought about Tom, wondering if he would take foolish chances. I listened to the gunfire. Would he be hit by some random bullet? I pictured bloodied bodies, torn limbs.

I set my burning cigarette in the ashtray, ripped the sheet of paper from the typewriter and tossed it into the wastebasket. Tom knew how to stay out of the gunfire, he'd said a million times. I clamped my eyes shut for a moment and then tightened the knots of my resolve. To the accompaniment of constant artillery fire, I inserted another sheet of paper into the cylinder, and tapped on the keys. I began with the children's evacuation piece. The Atocha Railroad Station. An hour or two went by as I wrote. The rumble of cannon fire never stopped. I hadn't yet finished the story when Tom burst into the room. I rose and greeted him with a tight hug. He was out of breath. "They're stopping them!"

"Who's stopping whom?"

"The people of Madrid are stopping the Nationalist's advance across the river on the Campo. Major Palacios led his two battalions of Republican militiamen in a counterattack. I was in the trench next to the Franceses Bridge when the militias crossed over it onto the Nationalists' left flank. I talked to the medics who were bringing back the wounded. They told me the fascists have been pushed back, in spite of their Italian and German tanks. But the losses were heavy they said. I just now went to the press briefing and the officer said the militias lost perhaps half their men, but Varela's Moroccan troops have been checked." Tom reached for the pitcher of water and poured himself a glass, which he thirstily drained. As he paused for breath I thought of the woman at the train station, the one with the schoolteacher husband. Would he be one of the men killed in the counterattack?

Tom set down the glass and lit a cigarette. "The International Brigades are in place there now on the Campo and apparently are suffering heavy losses, too. But they have Russian weapons. And artillery. The reporters who were there agreed that they're fighting like demons. Anthony was at the meeting and he told me the Brigaders are also holding the line in University City, to the north." Clamping his cigarette between his lips, squinting from the smoke in his eyes, Tom pulled his map from his hip pocket and spread it out on the table next to my typewriter. He set his cigarette next to mine in the ashtray. "The university is spread out over a large area."

I could see the squares indicating separate buildings, labeled engineering, medicine, philosophy etc. "An odd terrain for a battlefield. Were you close to the fighting?"

"For a short time." He indicated the mud on his clothes. "But I kept under cover, believe me. It was no picnic. And I stayed on this side of the river. Near the northern section of the front. Some of our soldiers' rifles were so old they could barely shoot. But they're fighting hard. If one militiaman is hit, there's another waiting to pick up the rifle and take over. It breaks your heart, but they're so brave, so determined, you can't help but be thrilled."

I noted Tom's term *our* soldiers. I understood now how he felt. Objectivity be damned. I wanted the fascists to lose, and not only for the sake of Spain. For all of us.

Tom gave me a hug. "I'm so relieved you got back here OK? Any problems?"

"None. And you can't know how glad I am to see you."

He glanced at my typewriter and the papers scattered on the table. "But you got some work done, I see."

"I've been writing up the evacuation piece."

"Great. I need to write up my story too—clean up. Then I'll go over to Telefonica to file it. I'll be back in an hour. Then we could go to Gaylord's, if you still want to. Plenty of sources of information there, I bet. All those Russians!"

6
Madrid
November, 1936

That evening the sounds of gunfire and artillery seemed louder than ever, but the sky was free of bombers. Tom and I walked quickly toward the Prado. Hotel Gaylord was between the Prado and Retiro Park on the edge of the Salamanca district, which had now become crowded with refugees. An end to the air-raid brought hundreds of people and animals out on the street. I passed one man, a farmer, leading a cow down the sidewalk. Four or five sheep were grazing in the park. The pungent smell of sheep and cow dung was mixed with the odor of gunpowder and cement dust.

As we entered the hotel we were struck by a clamor of raised voices. It didn't sound like the usual hotel lobby chatter. The atmosphere was jubilant. Men were making excited gestures with their hands, and the air was blue with cigarette smoke. In the center of the room I spied Pasionaria. She was speaking to a short, gray-haired man with horn-rimmed glasses dressed in gray britches and tunic and black leather boots. Tom nudged me and murmured into my ear that the man talking to Dolores Ibarruri was the Pravda correspondent, Mikhail Koltsov, "Stalin's eyes and ears."

Dolores glanced in my direction and her eyes lit with recognition. "Ah, it's the American girl, Margarita." Introductions were made, and Koltsov bowed over my hand, flashing a charming smile. We spoke in Spanish, although later Koltsov spoke to us in English. "Please, let me get you some vodka. And how about a little caviar?"

41

Both Tom and I laughed. "Yes, please! How wonderful." Koltsov brought us small plates of caviar spread on triangles of toast, and a waiter brought a tray with glasses, a bottle of vodka, and set it on a table next to us.

Koltsov raised his glass. "Here's to a Republican victory and Franco's defeat!"

We all tossed back our vodka. Koltsov immediately plucked the bottle from the tray and re-filled our glasses. "Have you heard that Varela's attack at the Casa de Campo has been checked?"

Tom nodded. "I was at the front by the Franceses Bridge today. I also heard that the Militias are holding off Castejon's column at University City."

Dolores lifted her chin in a defiant gesture. "But the XIth International Brigade is with them. And they fought bravely at the Campo, pushing back Serrano's column." Her expression darkened. "Many, many brave men perished."

I exchanged glances with Tom. He had told me that the Madrileños of the Mixed Brigades were the ones who stopped the Moroccans and Legionnaires. The International Brigades didn't get to the front until late in the day, well after the colonial advance had been stopped. I kept that thought to myself, however. This wasn't the time or place to contradict these fervent Party members—especially when I was drinking their vodka and tasting their luxurious caviar.

Dolores then explained that they'd been speaking about the Nationalist's fifth column.

"Fifth column?" I was confused. "I thought there were only four columns of colonial troops attacking Madrid."

Koltsov narrowed his eyes. "It's been reported General Mola said he'd sent four columns to take Madrid, but a fifth column was inside the city: the rich fascist insurgents in hiding. It's the Fifth Column we must now find and destroy."

Dolores pressed her lips together. "We will rout them out. Soldiers of the 5th Regiment are searching for the traitors at this moment."

I felt a shiver go up my spine. These people were fanatics. Another Inquisition? Communist instead of Catholic? I looked around the room at the excited men and women. Koltsov excused himself and bowed over my hand once more. Dolores took hold of my arm, beckoning to Tom, and introduced us to a cadaverously thin, sharp-eyed Spaniard, Arturo Barea. His face was narrow, his nose aquiline and his jet black hair was combed straight back. We spoke together in Spanish. I translated for Tom.

Nervously, Barea blew out a cloud of strong-smelling smoke. "We will get to know each other well," he said, smiling. "The Military Junta has decided that censorship of journalists' reports is necessary. Before you file your stories, you must present them to me or to my assistant, Ilsa Kulscar. Ilsa speaks fluent English. I, alas, can read English, but do not speak it. Only Spanish and French." He took another drag on his cigarette, holding it with nicotine-stained thumb and fingers. "Certain military information will be censored and we will insist that you do not mention the existence of Russian armaments. A representative of the Soviet government signed the non-intervention agreement, but Stalin has decided to circumvent it, just as Hitler and Mussolini have done."

I remembered hearing that millions in Spanish gold had been shipped to Russia for the purchase of armaments—and for safekeeping. The armaments sent by Stalin were purchased fairly.

A man in a dark suit approached Dolores. Alexander Orlov was his name. I had heard about him. He was the chief of the NKVD, Stalin's top spy in Madrid, and had a reputation for ruthlessness. At the slightest suspicion of opposition to Stalin he had dispatched men to Siberia or the firing squad. He wore a small, neatly clipped mustache, was even-featured, and his thin brown hair was beginning to recede at the temples. I guessed him to be in his late thirties. He didn't look at all cruel or dangerous. His looks didn't match his reputation.

Dolores turned to speak to him privately, but before she left me she suggested we meet the next day soon after daybreak. "I will have a car at my disposal. I want to inspect the front and speak to our brave soldiers. I also will visit the wounded—and my Catholic nuns. It will be a story for your Americans."

I thanked her profusely and agreed to meet her in front of the Florida in the morning.

As Tom and I were walking back to the Florida in the bluish light of the street lamps, with gunfire and artillery barrage as background noise and flamenco music drifting from shadowed doorways, I couldn't keep from thinking of what we'd heard about the Fifth Column—and censorship. I glanced up at Tom. "When Koltsov talks about destroying the people siding with the insurgents here in Madrid, do you think he means killing them?"

"Probably. It's what the fascists have done in places like Badajoz. It's a brutal war. None of them are sweethearts. fascists, Anarchists, Trotskyists. Stalinists."

I shook my head. "Then there's Hitler. Burning books, torturing, throwing Jews or anyone who opposes them into concentration camps. Pure evil. Sometimes I feel as if I were living on the edge of Hell, Dante's inferno." Tom put his arm around me. "And what about the censorship? I bet it won't just be Russian armaments you can't write about."

"You got that one right." Then he stopped in his tracks and turned me toward him. "Come on, Meg, let's change the subject. It's true we're in the midst of a war, but we're in Spain! The land of passion! Let's go to Chicote's for tapas and Spanish brandy. We'll drink to the brave, true men and women of Madrid who have fought off our enemies—and to those who died so valiantly. Before the bombing starts again. Then I want to go back to the hotel and make mad love to you."

Which is exactly what we did.

The air-raid began at dawn the next morning. In spite of the sounds of battle that continued throughout the night, the siren woke us from a sound sleep. Groggily we rolled out of bed. We quickly washed, dressed and descended the stairs to the cellar bar with our fellow sleep-deprived journalists. The exploding bombs shook the building and rattled the coffee cups, and I found myself listening intensely to the planes and explosions, trying to estimate their distance from the hotel. This was my third air-raid, the second day of the battle for Madrid, and I was learning to judge the raid's strength and its target. This one seemed to be targeting north of the city where the Brigaders were fighting.

I looked at my watch. Pasionaria said she'd be here soon after dawn, but I didn't think she'd be out during the bombing. I drank my coffee and chewed a chunk of stale bread the staff had assembled for us, listening for explosions. We didn't talk. Finally, the drone of the Junkers faded, the explosions became more distant and the all-clear siren sounded. I looked at Tom. "So, Tom, what perilous activity have you planned for today?"

"I'm not sure, but I think I'll go up to University City to check out what's happening there. And speaking of perilous activities, your going with Dolores to the front doesn't exactly sound like a picnic. If she's recognized by the fascists, she'd be an excellent target."

"She's a survivor. I'm sure she knows how to keep from being killed. She's been on the firing line so long. And her people will protect her." I looked at my watch again. "But now I better get outside. I don't want to miss her. It's an incredible opportunity for me."

Tom grinned. "Right. But I'll wait with you. I'm curious about the car she'll be in. I understand the protection on the so-called armored cars are thin as cardboard." He took hold of my arm as we went out the door.

I grinned back at him. "Thanks for being so reassuring!"

Out on the street the sound of artillery was louder, but people were streaming up the underground subway stairs on the corner, where they had sought safety during the bombing. Some were carrying blankets and pillows, indicating they'd slept there all night.

Tom watched the bleary-eyed parade of people walk by. "I'll have to remember to show that censor, Arturo Barea, my story when I write it up. What a bother. I'll have to find out where his office is. I forgot to ask last night."

At that moment, a rattling, old taxi pulled up in front of the hotel. Dolores leaned out the rear window and called to me. I smiled at Tom. So much for the armored car. All the city's taxis had been requisitioned by the military junta. I gave Tom a quick kiss and wished him luck.

"You too!" he whispered.

Dolores introduced me to the driver and the soldier sitting next to him, both soldiers of the 5th Regiment. She referred to me as Comarada Margarita, la periodista americana. The driver was Corporal Arturo and the soldier in the passenger seat was Sergeant Roberto. The muzzle of his rifle was protruding from the car window. "We're going to the Franceses Bridge," Dolores said. "The Dombrowski Battalion of the International Brigade is there. Mostly Poles, but I think we can understand each other. I want to congratulate them for what they're doing for Spain and democracy and the workers of the world."

As we drove through the section of Madrid near the river, I was dismayed to see the damage that had already been done by the bombs and artillery. The buildings had been abandoned. The street was covered in shards of brick and broken glass, which our driver tried to avoid. Sections of walls had fallen from the structures, revealing rooms of broken furnishings—bedsteads and dressers—covered in plaster dust. Windows were without glass. Smoke-stained curtains flapped against broken shutters. I pointed my Leica to the ruins and clicked the shutter. La Pasionaria nodded approvingly. "The world must learn of this destruction."

Drawing close to the front line, the noise of battle increased in volume: deep booming sounds of the artillery barrage, the rattle of machine guns, the sharp crack of rifle fire. Dolores' black eyes were scanning the street from left to right as we drove through the rubble, as if watching for an ambush. "The fighting was fierce all night long," she said. "Many losses. Many wounded. True brave men, all."

Corporal Arturo stopped the car when we reached a barricade made up of paving stones from the street, sandbags, and tattered mattresses. Three tanks covered in tree branches were parked behind a wall next to the barricade. Dolores eyed the tanks. "Russian tanks, Pavlov T-26s," she announced. "But no photographs, please."

I fished my notebook from my coat pocket and began to take notes. Dolores saw what I was doing, and said sternly, "you know you won't be able to identify the tanks as Russian."

"I know," I said. "The censor won't permit it, but I can describe the scene." I stared at the helmeted soldiers who were perched on top of the tanks and at the other soldiers whose heads poked up from the hatch openings. We were about a fifty yards away from the bridge. I could see the sandbagged trenches topped by barbed wire on either side of its entrance. The thunder of artillery grew louder. I scrawled the words *3 tanks, trenches, barbed wire, artillery* in my notebook. My hands were shaking.

We descended from the taxi onto the rubble-strewn street behind the barricade. I stepped over a child's broken doll. A soldier in the uniform of the International Brigade stepped forward and spoke gruffly in a language I assumed was Polish. Then his eyes lit up. "La Pasionaria!" he said and called out to an officer standing by the tank, who stepped forward, and recognizing Dolores, called out in Spanish, "La Pasionaria! Comarada!" He took hold of her hand and kissed it. He told us he spoke both Polish and Spanish. "But you must leave immediately. We are about to advance across the river with the tanks and my company of men." He pointed to the wall, where we could see the men in formation, their rifles held across their chests, ready to march forward. At that moment, following the sharp retort of a rifle, a bullet struck the wall next to us. I ducked my head, in an automatic response then peered up at the bullet hole in the wall and the masonry it had dislodged onto the dirt below. My heart was thumping. Reality had struck along with that bullet. People died here.

After a beat the officer continued. "Snipers are hidden amongst the trees in the Campo. The Nationalists have pulled back most of their men and tanks, but a machine-gun emplacement and the snipers continue to fire at us. We will take them out. Varela's artillery has been withdrawn to Mount Garibitas." He held out his binoculars to Dolores. "You can see the big cannons up there on the right. Their shells still reach this side of the river." I scribbled a few more words in my notebook and my hands shook so much I doubted they were legible.

Dolores took the glasses and peered into them. She held the binoculars with a steady hand. She was calm, unshaken by the sniper shot. Unlike me. My hands were trembling so that I had to stuff them into my pockets, along with notebook and pencil. "And the fighting to the north?" Dolores asked.

"The Mixed Brigades counterattacked, crossing the river at the San Fernando Bridge on Varela's left flank. They've been fighting all night. The Nationalists had to withdraw most of their troops and tanks from this section of the Campo to stop them. We're about to hit them from this side."

Dolores returned the glasses to the captain and then lithely stepped over rubble and a low barricade in her rope-soled shoes and walked toward the men who were about to face the enemy. She went from man to man, thanking them, wishing them luck, her head held high, her shoulders back. She looked like a queen reviewing her troops, a queen dressed in an old black skirt, woolen jacket and thick stockings. Most of the men were short, no taller than Dolores. Some were blond, blue-eyed, others Slavic and dark. What cataclysmic events in their past had brought these men to fight for Spain, I wondered.

Our two 5th Regiment escorts herded us back into the taxi and quickly drove off. Dolores ordered them to take us to the Palace Hotel, which was now serving as a hospital for the wounded. I forced myself to write a few more notes about what I'd seen. Unfortunately, the air-raid siren sounded again, and when I looked up at the sky I could see the line of Junkers on their approach, ready to drop their bombs. The little Russian Chatos were diving at them. Corporal Arturo raced the car to the first underground subway station and insisted we go down into the shelter.

We joined a crowd of women, children and the elderly. I helped one fragile, bent, gray-haired woman descend the stairs one step at a time into the gloomy cement tunnel. Most of the people recognized Dolores as soon as they heard her voice. "La Pasionaria! No Pasarán!" they called out.

She responded with the Republican clenched fist salute and "no pasarán!"

We settled on the platform's cement floor and leaned back against the cold wall. Next to me was a woman clutching a sleeping baby. People sat quietly on the few benches or on the floor, wide-eyed with apprehension, listening to the sound of the distant explosions. The tunnel smelled of dust, damp and a faint whiff of urine. The platform was only twenty feet or so wide on either side of the tracks. "I'd hate to have to stay here all night," I said, turning to Dolores.

She shrugged. "I've been in worse. Prisons dirtier, smellier, more crowded." She reached into her leather portfolio and brought out a cloth-wrapped package containing chunks of bread and cheese. She broke off a piece of bread and handed it to me. She then cut off slices of the cheese with a sharp knife she had pulled from her bag. "Eat while we have the chance," she said, placing the pieces of cheese on the cloth she had spread on her lap. "This place reminds me of prison, and the thought of prison reminds me of hunger."

As I took a bite of the bread and cheese, I thought about what I knew of Dolores' past. Not a lot. I realized this would be the time to ask my questions. "Dolores, I know a little about you—that you're from a mining region in the Basque country, a miner's daughter, and a wife of a miner. You were elected Deputy from Asturias to the Cortes in January of this year. You've had six children, only two surviving."

She sighed. "Yes. And those two are now being educated in Russia so that I can devote my full energy to my work. The deaths of my babies broke my heart. My husband's wages were often not enough to pay the rent. We ate a few potatoes instead of meat. When the babies were sick we had no money for a doctor. Life was hard. Very, very hard." She picked up her knife and grasped it firmly. "The miners were worked to death for a pittance, and when men like my husband, Julian Ruiz, attended political meetings or helped organize a strike, they were thrown into prison. The life of my parents and my own family was like a deep pit, without horizons, where the light of sun never reached."

I wondered where her husband was now, but hesitated to ask. "And when you were a child, were you able to attend school?"

"Oh yes. We were sent to a kindergarten at an early age. My mother gave birth to eleven children. I was the eighth. Women like my mother were domestic slaves. For one peseta a day, the teacher freed our mothers from the need to care for their small children." With a swift motion she cut each of us another piece of cheese. "I learned to read and write quite young. When I went to elementary school I was taught by the sisters and priests—a lot of religious mumbo jumbo, but I was a devout Catholic."

The baby on the woman's lap next to me began to wail. The mother hastily put the child to her breast. Other children cried fretfully. I glanced at Dolores. Her neck was taut, strong, as if it was accustomed to holding her head proudly. "But you left the Church." I said, wanting her to continue.

"Indeed. As a girl I was deeply religious. I sometimes helped the sisters clean and decorate the church. One day I happened to look up from my task just as two sisters of Charity were changing the robes on the statue of the Virgin, whom I worshiped passionately. Underneath the embroidered petticoats the sisters were removing, I saw the sticks the statue was made of—like a scarecrow in the fields. It was a shock that changed my life. The trappings of the church were just that. Nothing substantive underneath." She tore the remaining piece of bread in two chunks and handed me one. "People were starving, the priests toadied to the rich, God didn't care, the Holy Mother was a sham. The priests preached to us to accept our poverty while they amassed vast wealth. They watched us weep for our dead babies and told us we should rejoice, that our children were now angels in heaven."

And so, I thought, you now worship Stalin and the Communist Party instead of the Catholic God. While she had been talking, we continued to hear thudding sounds as bombs hit the city. They seemed distant. The subway station was two stories down into the earth. At each deep boom, people cried out, clutched their children close. The raid seemed to take longer than yesterday's. I wondered if the dread German Condor Legion had been put into action. I shivered, thinking of Tom, hoping he'd found a place to shield himself from the bombing.

Dolores was listening to the explosions. "At least as a miner's daughter I am used to dynamite. And I know its power. During summer holidays from school we children would wander freely. Our mothers were too busy with younger children or trying to eke out a living to be concerned about us. We'd jump onto moving railroad box cars, run through abandoned mining tunnels, climb over piles of rubble, slide down inclined planes. Our playground was treacherous, but it prepared us for the hard life ahead."

"How old were you when you were married?"

"Twenty. I had been working as a domestic for three years and wanted my own home. But my mother warned me. After a few days of happiness comes the icy reality of existence. Like the song. 'Madre, que cosa es casar? Hija, hilar, parir y llorar. Mother, what is marriage? Daughter, marriage is weaving, giving birth, weeping.' Weeping for our impotence, weeping for our dying children." As she spoke, she smiled ironically but without self-pity. I didn't know how to respond. This woman had suffered and yet had become strong.

A subway train clattered up to the platform and a few people boarded. When the rumble of the departing train subsided, she continued. "My husband was in jail much of the time for his union organizing work. In 1920 I read Karl Marx and joined the Communist Party. I began to write for the miner's newspaper, signing myself as Pasionaria, after the flower of that name. I had four pregnancies. My first boy died an infant, the second, Ruben, survived and is in Russia. I gave birth to triplets the same year that Primo de Rivera became Dictator. Only one of the triplets survived, Amaya. My last little girl died in infancy also. And I wept, just as the song said I would." She turned to me calmly. "My story is not unique. Suffering was the norm amongst the workers in the mines and factories, the peasants in the fields. For their women the life was intolerable. Spanish men can be tyrants to their wives. Since then I have been doing all I possibly can to improve women's conditions, to provide health care, to help them be free."

I was moved by her story of poverty and loss. It was a tale I'd never forget, I was sure. Again I wondered about her husband, but she didn't speak of him. I forced myself to continue my interview. "And when were you elected to the Central Committee of the Spanish Communist Party?"

"In 1930. I had been elected to the provincial committee of the Basque Communist Party in 1920 when I was twenty-five years old and my husband was in prison. I became politically very active. In 1930, when I became a member of the Central Committee I moved to Madrid with my surviving children, Ruben and Amaya, and became editor of the Mundo Obrero, the Worker's World. In 1931 I was arrested and was in prison for two years. Friends and relatives cared for my two children."

My notebook was in my pocket and I wanted desperately to jot down notes about her story. I had feared doing so might be inhibiting, but I knew I would not remember the dates if I didn't write them down. I quietly pulled out the notebook and took notes. As I was reviewing in my mind what I'd seen and what Dolores had told me, the all-clear siren sounded. We rose from the bench, stretched and plodded with the crowd to the stairs that would take us into to the light of day.

The light was blinding when Dolores and I reached the top of the subway stairs. It took a few seconds for my eyes to get used to the glare. At first glance it seemed that that no bombs had fallen here, at least. A yellowish layer of smoke clung to the rooftops, but the buildings had not been damaged. The street was covered with a film of ash. On the horizon to the north black smoke was rising into the sky. I could see flickers of flame. The air smelled of smoke, gunpowder, and I could taste ash and the grit of masonry on my tongue. "They were bombing the working class district," Dolores said, somberly. "I hope the people took shelter."

Sgt Roberto was waiting for us by the stair railing. He escorted us to the taxi parked half a block away. "To the Salamanca District," Dolores directed, "I'll tell you where to go when we get to the Prado." She turned to me. "We will stop to see the nuns for a few minutes. I want you to tell the world about what you see. Then we'll go to the hospital at the Palace Hotel."

Good, I thought. The Salamanca District. Franco had said they wouldn't bomb it. Since Koltsov had told us about the alleged existence of the Fifth Column, I had been wondering if its members lived in the Salamanca. It was the exclusive neighborhood of Madrid where the rich had built mansions as well as where the foreign embassies were located.

As we drove through the city, I reflected upon what Dolores had told me about her troubled life. I was surprised she felt protective toward her nuns, especially after what she'd said about the Church. I knew she had met Stalin at the Moscow Comintern meeting last year. At that meeting Stalin changed the Communist Party line to accommodate the Western democracies. The Communists would now make alliances with other parties who were anti-fascist. They would also tolerate freedom of religion, and Stalin insisted upon Party discipline.

Now Dolores gave Corporal Arturo directions to the nuns' house, and turning to me said, "the right-wing newspapers in Europe depict me as a monster, that I murder nuns and priests, whereas the truth is I protect them when I can. You will see. Those poor sisters were in hiding, terrified of being discovered. By accident, some soldiers of the 5th Regiment found them. The soldiers had been looking in the Salamanca district for a house to use as a headquarters. When one of the nuns answered the door she fainted when she saw the soldiers. She was convinced she would be raped, tortured, killed, but the 5th Regiment soldiers convinced her and the other sisters in the house that they would not hurt them. In fact, they would provide protection. They nailed a sign on the front door saying the house was under the protection of the 5th Regiment and gave the nuns a document that stated the same."

We were now passing the Prado museum, which I saw had been sandbagged, the windows boarded up. The government buildings nearby were also sandbagged. Dolores continued with her tale. "The soldiers then informed me and asked me to call on the sisters, which I did. I suggested they might be able to do some productive work. They offered to do nursing or teaching, but I knew that the sick or wounded of Madrid or the Brigades—or parents—would not trust nuns, so I proposed they do some sewing, making children's clothes for the orphans and the evacuees. I would bring them the materials to work with. They happily agreed, and that's what they've been doing since then."

When we arrived at the house and I saw the notice nailed to the carved wooden door, I photographed it. A nun greeted Dolores with a happy cry, and we were immediately surrounded by chattering Sisters, all talking at once. They pointed to the stacks of children's clothes they had made. Dolores told them someone would come for them in the next few days. "I just stopped by to make sure you had everything you need."

They assured us they were fine and were well taken care of. We bade them good-bye and returned to the taxi, where Dolores told Corporal Arturo to take us to the hospital at the Palace Hotel on the Plaza de Cortes. He pulled up before an ornately decorated building. Two old vans with red crosses painted on their sides were parked in front of us. Medical orderlies were carrying a wounded boy on a stretcher into the hotel. He didn't look more than sixteen. He had thick, black curly hair poking out from a bloodied cloth tied about his head. His shirt at his shoulder was wet with blood, and as Dolores and I mounted the marble stairs leading to the front doors I saw a trail of black-edged blood. Inside the double doors the large space that was once a lobby smelled of ether and urine and sweat. The floor was covered with men lying on makeshift stretchers or mats, their wounds wrapped in strips of cloth. Their moans and cries broke my heart. The boy who had just been carried in was crying, "Mama, Mama me duele." The orderlies carried him into an elevator. The doors shut on his cries.

A man nearby reached out his hand and called out for water. I knelt beside him and told him I'd fetch some. He then closed his eyes and seemed to lose consciousness. His leg was splinted with a stick and wrapped with what looked like strips of a bloodied shirt.

I searched the room for a nurse—or someone to ask for water. Several women with nurses' head coverings and some uniformed men were bending over the wounded. Orderlies carried men on stretchers to the elevators. I assumed the doctors were operating on the upper floors or perhaps in the basement. What I was witnessing was the triage. As I stood by the man who had asked me for water and who seemed now to be unconscious, a nurse rushed to his side, knelt beside him, examined his leg and then called for the orderlies to carry the man to the elevators. She looked up at me. "We have no morphine. They pass out with the pain." She hurried off to another groaning man on a stretcher.

I turned to Dolores. She was talking to a man whose head was partially wrapped in bandages, but who was sitting in one of the hotel's high-backed brocaded chairs under a crystal chandelier. "The fighting is fierce at University City," he said in a hoarse, exhausted voice, "but we're holding the line." He spoke Spanish with a foreign accent.

She patted him on the shoulder and thanked him for being here. "Where are you from?"

"Paris," he said. "The XIth International Brigade."

She told him how proud she was of the Brigade and how she knew they would bring freedom to Spain and save the world from fascism. She then turned to me. "I have a meeting at the Ministry, but first I need to find Major Gomez, the officer in charge of the medical unit. I need to report to the Junta. I can drop you off at your hotel, if you like." She spoke in her usual business-like manner.

"Dolores, thank you for taking me with you today. You can't know how grateful I am, but I need to walk, absorb what I've seen and heard today. My hotel is only a few blocks away." Actually, I felt like bursting into tears. The moans of the wounded made my heart squeeze shut. The reality of the war, its blood and pain and death had finally shown its ugly face to me. So much of the time in Madrid the war had seemed distant. Daily life had gone on. Streetcars ran on their tracks, the subway trains functioned, people drank vodka and brandy and went to tapa bars. As I stepped out the door, another wounded boy on a stretcher was being carried up the stairs. He, too, was in pain crying for his mother. My legs felt weak, and for a moment I feared I would vomit. Suddenly I thought about Tom. He was at University City. He could easily be hit by shrapnel or stray bullets. The distant booming of artillery continued. I found myself racing toward the Florida.

7
Madrid
November, 1936

As I dashed down the darkening street to the Florida, I couldn't stop thinking of the wounded soldiers, of their cries for help. I prayed that Tom had returned from University City in one piece. I burst through the hotel door into the atrium, glanced at the bar, and stopped to catch my breath. Thank God. Tom was leaning against the bar talking to an English engineer I had met briefly the day before. "Tom," I called, as I ran toward him. "You're OK!"

"And you're OK," Tom said, laughing, hugging me.

"Actually, I'm only partially OK. I could do with a brandy. I was just at the Palace Hotel, which they've made into a hospital for the wounded. It was heartrending. I was afraid you might be among them."

"No, luck was with me, and I'm pretty good at hitting the ground in a split second, believe me." He turned to the bartender and ordered a brandy for me. "Meg, have you met Christopher Lance?"

We shook hands. "Yes, we met yesterday by the stairs. Anthony introduced us."

He smiled. "During the afternoon artillery shelling." He was tall with the shoulders of a tennis player. His eyes were ice blue, and his brown hair was neatly combed. He was wearing a brown leather jacket over a blue cashmere sweater. I guessed he'd be in his late twenties, about the same age as Tom. He spoke with a plummy British accent. He'd lived in Madrid two years, working for a British engineering company, he told us. His flat had been hit by an artillery shell and his wife had gone back to England. He'd just moved into the Florida while the British Embassy fixed up a place for him there. "So the Palace Hotel has been transformed into a hospital?"

I nodded. "And it's filling up with wounded."

Tom scowled. "The Moroccans are firing new machine guns and the Italians are manning their Fiat tanks. Today I saw men of the XIth Brigade carrying rifles manufactured in Switzerland in 1886. It seems hopeless." He turned to Lance. "Did you hear the Non-Intervention Committee's report about their conclusions?"

"Yes. They found no evidence of foreign armaments being used here in Spain. Europe will not interfere. They're remaining neutral."

"Incredible!" I shouted. "And what are those bombs and shells falling on us from the German Junkers and Italian fighter planes and tanks."

"And the Soviet fighter planes and tanks," Lance said, quietly. "And General Goriev? The Communists are the ones who scare Britain and France."

I glanced quickly at Tom. Who was this Lance? Was he a fascist sympathizer, pro-Franco? Or as a neutral had he been able to keep from taking sides? Anthony had told me the British in Madrid leaned politically to the right. I set my brandy glass onto the bar and said coolly, "it would seem you're able to maintain your objectivity."

"I try. Unlike many of you journalists." He gave me a charming smile.

I replied with a touch of ice in my voice. "I also try, but sometimes fascists make it difficult. Tom, I need to get cleaned up. I'll see you later." I nodded to Lance and headed for the stairs.

Tom caught up with me. He unlocked the door of my room with my key and closed it tightly behind us. I unbuttoned my coat and tossed it on the bed. "An odd one, Lance. He's different from the British reporters we know."

"Yeah, before you came in he was talking about the Russians and their obsession with the Fifth Column. He thinks they'll set off another wave of atrocities."

"Well, he certainly doesn't seem very upset about the Non-Intervention Committee's findings."

Tom took off his coat and pulled me close. " No, he doesn't. But forget about Lance. I'm just glad you're here. Safe. So tell me about La Pasionaria. What did you find out? And did she take you to the front? I was worried."

I thought of the bullet hitting the wall, the faces of the Poles, Dolores' grim story—and then the hospital. "It was all a shock, Tom. Reality in all its ugliness. Sometimes here in Madrid, when we're eating caviar with the Russians, riding the subway, ordering tapas and brandy at Chicotes, I forget there's a war. Today I felt like the scales dropped from my eyes. Nothing in my life in California prepared me for what I saw today."

Tom spoke with intensity. "I don't think anything can prepare you for this war. It's ugly, cruel, tragic. I might have seen the same wounded as you did. I watched as orderlies put the bloodied men and boys into the ambulances. What gets to me is how brave, how determined, and with what passion these men face the Nationalists. And they don't have decent weapons or sufficient ammunition. They don't have a chance in hell to win and yet Varela's troop has been pushed back. Then someone like Lance acts as though the Non-Intervention pact isn't a betrayal, isn't a short-sighted, tragic mistake." As he spoke he was pacing the floor between the window and the table. His expression was tense, angry. Abruptly, he snatched the pack of Luckies from the table and offered me one. "Sorry, Meg, I'm ranting. This war makes me so angry. I didn't mean to interrupt you. So where did Dolores take you? Did you meet any of the International Brigade?"

We propped ourselves against the headboard of the bed, lit our cigarettes and placed an ashtray between us. I told him what I had seen and heard at the front. I described the Polish Brigaders and the three Russian tanks. "You can use that in your story, but I know you won't be able to say they're Pavlov T-26 tanks."

Tom sighed. "I know. I took today's report to Barea—in duplicate, as instructed. He has an office at Telefonica, and another at the Foreign Ministry. It's on the fifth floor at Telefonica. At first he wanted me to pick it up tomorrow, but I told him I had a daily news report to broadcast. He was quite cooperative, said he'd put it on top of the pile and have it ready for me by the time my call went through. All the foreign reporters have to submit their stories to him. Then he stamps it and gives the duplicate copy to one of the switchboard censors fluent in the language its written. He's on the line wearing earphones when I call in our stories. He reads what we've written and listens to make sure we don't change anything. I met the guy who listened to me. He was in the office next to the booth. He's friendly enough, but it feels strange."

"I'll bet."

"I'll get used to it. But look, you saw the tanks. What else? Where were you during the air-raid?"

I skimmed through a description of the air-raid and Dolores' life story, the visit to the nuns and the hospital. "But, Tom, I'd like to go for a walk, get some fresh air—something to eat, maybe."

Tom looked at his watch. "It's too early for dinner at the Gran Via. Let's go to Chicote's before the bombing begins again."

I thought about listening to the mid-day explosions from the metro station and how I wondered if the planes were part of the Condor Legion. "Was today's bombing done by the Condor Legion?"

"No, but everyone predicts they'll be in action momentarily. At the press briefing this afternoon they told us the fighting is still fierce on the northern edge of the Campo." As he spoke I listened to the artillery shelling, which sounded like a distant thunderstorm. Tom stubbed out his cigarette and continued. "Varela's troops are being pushed back, but they continue to counterattack. And the Brigades are having a tough time at University City. Besides the wounded being loaded into ambulances I saw the dead bodies being piled onto trucks. It's a bloody mess, believe me. Carnage. And there's a shortage of morphine—along with everything else. But at least the Russian artillery is in place. Voronov was on the tower of Telefonica today. He and Colonel Mendoza have established an observation post up there. They're in control of the artillery."

As I listened to Tom's news, I thought about Lance's implied complaint about the help the Russians were providing to the Republicans—and his concern about their response to the threat of the Fifth Column. "Tom, did anyone at the briefing ask about Franco sympathizers in Madrid—the ones who might take part in an uprising from within the city?"

"There were a couple of questions, but Barea dodged them. 'It was being investigated,' he said. Actually, after we get something to eat I'd like to go to Gaylords again. Maybe we can pick up some clues about what the Russian investigation consists of."

It was dark on the Gran Via except for the blue-painted streetlights. They cast a light like moonlight on the lacy wrought iron balconies above our heads. When we entered Chicotes, Ralph Fitzgerald hailed us. A guitarist was playing a flamenco lament. Ralph indicated we join him at a nearby table. He put his arm across my shoulder. "So, baby, are you still hanging out with this NBC hack? If he bores you, you know where to find me."

"Hey, Ralph, watch it!" Tom said, grinning.

The waiter appeared and took our order for drinks and tapas. "I just filed my piece to the Trib," Ralph said, tossing back his brandy. "I was afraid the phone lines would be kaput, but I got through OK."

Tom frowned. "I didn't realize there was a problem."

"I was afraid there might be. The phone lines here in Madrid have been cut, but the cables to Paris and London are working fine, and the censor was listening on an extension in the next office. So my call went through."

"Did the exchange get hit?"

"Not that anyone knows. There's a rumor going around that the Defense Junta ordered the local lines cut off to prevent the Nationalist sympathizers from phoning their allies in the suburbs. That Fifth Column scare."

"Nobody said anything about it at the press briefing."

Ralph laughed. "Maybe they didn't know! Probably the 5th Regiment did it. Ordered by Goriev—or Orlov. Those Russians are paranoid. The 5th Regiment is now in charge of security. I hear most of the Civil Guard is being moved to Valencia."

Tom and I exchanged glances. We needed to go to Gaylord's. Maybe Dolores would be there and would know what the story was. She seemed to trust me. We finished our drinks and what remained of the tapas and took leave of Ralph.

Tom grinned at me. "Maybe they'll offer us caviar and vodka again. I'm still hungry. The tapas were skimpy and not very good. Madrid is running out of food, I'm afraid."

It was raining lightly as we walked down the Gran Via, and a chill wind blew from the mountains of the Guadarrama. Tom pulled his brown fedora down over his brow, and I tied a blue wool scarf over my head. We huddled close in the dark, damp night. I thought of the soldiers in the trenches, wet, muddy and scared. An occasional shot rang out, but the artillery had stopped firing. People rushed by, hurrying to get out of the rain and home before the bombing began again. A trolley rattled down the street. "How bizarre to see trolleys still running in the midst of a battle," I said.

"I took one today," Tom said. "To University City. Workers keep repairing the tracks. The trolley goes all the way to the front. When you see the trenches you get off! Bizarre indeed."

I thought of the Shattuck Avenue streetcar I used to take to go to the Oakland Gazette from Berkeley. It was shabby, boring, sometimes crowded. Who could imagine riding a streetcar to get to the front?

Now we'd arrived at Gaylord's. I felt safe here. No bombs, no artillery shells. The hotel lobby was buzzing with a mix of languages; Spanish, Russian, English and others I didn't recognize. The air was blue with the strong-smelling smoke of Russian cigarettes. Many of the men were in uniform. The few women were plainly dressed. I scanned the crowd as I removed the scarf from my head and we checked our wet coats. Dolores in her black skirt and jacket stood next to a table loaded with serving dishes and bottles I assumed were of vodka. She was talking to Pravda's Koltsov and a Spanish officer.

I glanced into the mirror by the door and pushed the damp hair out of my face. I straightened my checked wool skirt and decided I was presentable enough. We stepped into the crowded room, and as we drew near Dolores and Koltsov, she called out to us. "Margarita, Tomás, come and meet Major Mendez."

Dolores introduced them as the periodistas americanas de radio NBC.

The major bowed over my hand, kissing it lightly, and continued to hold it as he spoke. "Ah, the American girl with the astonishing blue eyes! Encantada."

I didn't know quite how to respond to this greeting. I withdrew my hand and replied with the usual "mucho gusto". I guessed he was in his early thirties and had the features of a Spanish patrician painted by Velásquez: narrow nose and face, dark, lively eyes and fair skin. He spoke an educated, beautiful Castillian.

"I noticed you here yesterday evening," he continued with a flirtatious smile, "when you were speaking to Comrade Dolores. I asked her about you. Your appearance in this chilly room is as warming as a ray of sunshine."

"Thank you," I said. The man was a charmer but I was familiar with that brand of charm. Obviously, flirtations continued, even in the midst of war—or perhaps especially during a war. I noted the major's use of *comrade*, which meant he was probably a Party member. It still surprised me when members of the aristocracy became Communists. Did they smell the winner? Or did they genuinely believe in the Communist doctrine? I was saved from continuing the conversation by Tom, who handed me a glass of vodka and a canapè of caviar.

The two men shook hands. "Señor Koltsov tells me you are a member of the Defense Junta and are in charge of weapon procurement and distribution," Tom said.

"Correct. At the moment a difficult task."

"I'm sure it is." Tom took a sip of his vodka.

"But more tanks are arriving, "Dolores said, "and artillery. From Soviet Russia."

I eyed Major Mendez. He was a member of the Junta. I thought of the telephone lines being cut, and that Ralph had suggested that it might have been ordered by the Defense Junta—to impede any plot being organized by the so-called Fifth Column. I wondered if Mendez would know if that were the case. Did I dare ask?

Koltsov was praising the bravery and skill of the International Brigades. "Now if we can find and eliminate the Fifth Column, I'm certain we can hold Madrid." His smile was almost complacent, but the word *eliminate* seemed to remain frozen in the air. I looked at Tom. A waiter was offering him another glass of vodka. Tom declined then said to Koltsov, "you must know the Madrid phones aren't functioning. One of our colleagues has suggested the lines were cut off by order of the Defense Junta. Do you know if this is true?"

Koltsov gave Mendez a questioning look. Mendez nodded. "Yes, it's not a secret. It's a strategy to prevent fascist sympathizers from contacting their fellow-plotters in the suburbs, the Fifth Column." Mendez' expression hardened. "We will find the vermin and exterminate them immediately. Telephone service will be restored within a few days.

The city of Madrid will remain in Republican hands. We have already moved the Civil Guard to Valencia. In Badajoz some of the Guard switched sides during a Nationalist attack. That will not happen in Madrid. And at this moment we are beginning the removal of the insurgent prisoners from the Madrid prison to another site."

Tom's eyes flickered. He spoke slowly. "Are you at liberty to tell us where?"

"No, I'm sorry." He bowed to us both and walked away. I watched him join Orlov, the NKVD head spy.

Tom looked at his watch then suggested we depart. I thanked Dolores once more for taking me with her on her day's tasks. She assured me I was welcome to go with her at any time.

As we were leaving Gaylord's Tom took my arm. "Meg, I really want to go out to the Model Prison to see if I can find out what's going on. It's still early, only 8:30."

"Do you know where it is?"

"It's up Calle Princesa. It's a block from the Moncloa subway station."

I was no longer famished because of the caviar I'd eaten and I wanted to go along with Tom. "I'll come with you," I blurted. You might not find people who speak any of your languages."

Tom gave me a searching look. "OK. Why not? It shouldn't be dangerous. They won't let us inside, but maybe we can talk to someone who knows where the new prison is. We'll take the subway. There's a station across the street."

The rain had stopped, but it was dark and cold, and we could still hear the sounds of artillery shells exploding in the distance. This section of the city wasn't being targeted at the moment. The street was jammed with trucks and horse-drawn wagons. An accident had caused the traffic to backup, and as we crossed the street, threading our way around the vehicles and horses, we passed close to an ambulance. When I glanced at the driver I realized it was Lance. "Tom, look isn't that Christopher Lance?"

Tom tapped gently at the window and called a greeting. Lance seemed not to recognize us at first. He then raised his hand in a wave, but did not roll down the window. He turned away from us and inched his ambulance forward. Tom grasped my hand and we continued on our way. "I didn't know Lance was an ambulance driver," he said.

"No, he didn't mention it. He's probably taking the wounded to the hospital at the Palace Hotel."

Tom glanced at me and frowned. "Odd, most ambulance drivers are members of the Brigade. Lance didn't seem the type. He certainly isn't a Communist."

No, he surely was not. Odd, indeed, and hadn't he sounded surprised to hear the Palace Hotel had been turned into a hospital for the wounded?

We had reached the subway entrance. We descended the stairs and stepped around families camped on the floor wrapped in blankets or hunched over chunks of bread or botas of wine. They were here for the night, waiting for the Condor Legion and the Luftwaffe. A train pulled up to the platform and we climbed aboard, pushing our way into the crowded car.

The platform of the Plaza Moncloa subway station was even more crowded than that of the Gran Via and smelled of sweat, spilled wine and damp woolens. Spent air gusted from the gloomy, dark tunnels and the cement floor was hard under our feet, but these Madrileños were sheltered from the expected air-raid. We climbed the stairway into the chill air, which seemed fresh after the close atmosphere of the underground, but smelled faintly of granite dust, gunpowder and smoke. The artillery firing had stopped, however, and the night was strangely quiet. The sky had cleared and a full moon cast a pale light on the wet pavement.

As we crossed the plaza we spied the high cement wall and black metal gate of the Model Prison. We had just reached the sidewalk that faced the wall when the doors of the gate swung open, and two tarpaulin-covered trucks emerged. Uniformed guards carrying rifles stood on the running boards, but the tarpaulins hid the contents of the trucks from view. I fixed my eyes on the trucks as I watched them disappear into the darkness. The gates to the prison clanged shut.

"The prisoners, I bet," Tom murmured.

We crossed the street and approached the gate. Two armed men in dark blue coveralls and peaked caps were on guard. They both wore the Anarchist red and black scarves around their necks. One of them stepped forward and asked for our IDs. We handed him our papers and he eyed them carefully, peering into our faces, comparing them to the pictures on the documents. He nodded, smiled, and gave them back to us. "Periodistas, americanas. Bienvenidos a la Republica." He held up his clenched fist in the Republican salute. His cap had the letters FAI-CNT marked on its emblem, which I knew to indicate he was a member of the Federation of Anarchists. Tom offered him a Lucky Strike cigarette, which the guard accepted with enthusiasm. Tom then held out the pack of cigarettes to the second guard.

After lighting the cigarettes, the guard explained to his partner that we were journalists. Tom then asked me to question them about the governor of the prison. What was his name and when would it be possible to speak to him.

"The governor isn't here at the moment. And visiting hours are over. You will have to come back tomorrow." I translated what he had said and continued as interpreter during Tom's questioning.

"Well, can you tell us if the trucks we saw leaving the prison just now were carrying political prisoners to another prison site? And if they were, could you tell us where the other prison is located?"

The guard shot his co-worker a troubled glance, as if he were uncertain about the answer Tom's question. "One moment," he said. The two men drew some distance away from us and spoke rapidly to one another. I couldn't make out what they were saying, but whatever it was, their gestures and facial expressions indicated they were fearful and not in agreement.

The first guard returned to us and said that it was true that the prisoners were being shifted to another location, but he wasn't at liberty to say where. "Another two truckloads of prisoners were moved earlier today." He avoided eye contact with us as he spoke.

"Can you tell me how many political prisoners this facility holds?"

"About 2,000, but only 1,000 are being evacuated. The most important ones."

Tom pulled out his notebook and scribbled some numbers. "But you can't tell us where."

The guard's lips tensed. "No, and now you should leave." He saluted once more and returned to his post at the gate.

Reluctantly, we left. We walked slowly across the plaza toward the subway station. I hated the thought of descending into the crowded, smelly tunnels. The wind had died and the air had warmed somewhat. There was still no sign of bombers and the artillery was quiet. "Let's sit a moment." I indicated a wrought iron bench next to the path. "What did you think of those guards?"

Tom fished the pack of Luckies from his pocket, offered me one, and cupping his hand around the flame, lit first mine then his own. "They know much more than they were telling us. And they're afraid."

Suddenly, I heard a low whistle, then someone calling to us in a whispering voice. We both turned toward a darkened kiosk a few feet away from our bench. The voice had come from the shadows behind it. Tom took my arm and we stood up, ready to flee. "What do you want?" Tom said quietly in his stumbling Spanish. "Who are you?"

"A friend. I have something to tell you. Walk slowly toward me but stop when I say so."

I translated for Tom in a low voice, trailing behind him, clutching his hand. We stepped cautiously toward the shadowed kiosk. The voice told us to stop. I felt certain it was the voice of the prison guard at the gate. "Ask him what he wants to tell us." Tom said quietly. I did so and acted as translator for the rest of the encounter.

The man's answer was harsh, abrupt. "They're shooting the prisoners. Killing them."

"And who is doing the shooting?"

"Prison guards. Communists. On orders from top Party officials."

"And where?"

"Near Paracuellos de Jarama. Next to a freshly dug ditch. That's all I can say. Adios." Then he vanished.

In shocked silence, Tom and I moved woodenly toward the Moncloa subway station. We weren't able to talk about what we had heard until we emerged onto the Gran Via. My gut felt as if it had received a powerful kick. I felt sick. The guard had told the truth, I was certain. I was equally certain that we couldn't do anything with the information. The story had to remain untold. It would be too damaging to the anti-fascist cause. In low voices, Tom and I quickly conferred about what to do. We agreed we could not even hint we'd been told an atrocity was occurring, but we'd quietly keep our ears open for more information.

We sat side by side on the subway train, but didn't speak. We were both too troubled. When we arrived at the Gran Via Hotel for our evening meal, and descended into the noisy, smoke-filled cellar dining hall, we found almost every seat was occupied. Tom and I had to sit at separate tables. Could I possibly keep up a normal conversation with these sharp-eyed, voluble journalists while I was still in a state of shock, feeling like a conspirator? The waiter brought me the night's fare, lentil soup. I wasn't hungry but forced myself to eat. In this business I had to keep up my strength.

I exchanged introductions with the man on my left, who immediately continued an argument with his neighbor in French. They spoke too rapidly for me to follow. On my right was Arthur Koestler, whom I had already met. He was a reporter for the British liberal paper, *the News Chronicle*, and spoke English with an accent. He was originally from Budapest and was fluent in several languages. He gave me a charming smile. "Dining at the Gran Via is not like it used to be," he said, glancing at the soup. "And it will probably get worse. It seems as though all that's in their larder are lentils and dried-up salami."

I returned his smile. Koestler had a sympathetic face: thin, a little gaunt, but warm brown eyes, prominent nose and pronounced chin. I guessed he'd be in his early thirties. I'd heard he'd been banned from entering Nationalist Spain. I didn't know why and wanted to ask him about it, but didn't know how to begin. "It seems as though the Militias and the Brigades are holding the line," I said, which was a kind of Madrid reporter's small talk.

Koestler laughed. "Thank God. I was about to catch a ride to the coast until I heard about Varela's troops being pushed back. Franco would have me shot."

Now was my chance. "I was told Franco forbids you from entering Nationalist territory."

"Correct. In fact, he's now forbidden all journalists from English liberal papers from Nationalist territory. He objected to my writing about what I saw."

"Atrocities?"

"Yes, but that wasn't all. Last month I published a piece about the Italian and German military support in Nationalist Seville soon after the fascist uprising." He picked up his glass of red wine and took a sip. "I wrote about what I saw: German planes, tanks and personnel, Italian tanks and a great many Italian soldiers. It was estimated there were 20,000. It's clear that Hitler and Mussolini are preparing for a war with the Western democracies. They're using Spain to break in their troops. And I said that in my story. I also personally witnessed Nationalists shooting captured Republican Militamen."

"You were in Germany after Hitler took over. You must have also witnessed Nazi atrocities." I was becoming familiar with this word. Too familiar.

"I did, indeed. And I am a member of the German Communist Party, which makes me a persona non grata there—and now in Nationalist Spain. I barely escaped being shot in Seville."

"So what happened?"

"I had been interviewing the insurgent General Quiepo de Llano, who didn't know about my Party membership. As I left de Llano's office, a man who was waiting to speak to him recognized me from Berlin. It was Strindberg's son, a Nazi. He informed de Llano I was a member of the German Communist Party. Because I was a Communist, a Red, orders were issued for my immediate arrest as a spy. I managed to cross the border to Gibralter just in time." He spooned up the last of his soup. "My pamphlet was published in Paris in September. Franco must have read it—or heard about it. A few days after its publication liberal English journalists were banned from his territory. The piece was called *Espagne Ensanglantre*, Spain, covered in blood."

I thought of the bloodied wounded I'd seen at the hospital that day—and a certain freshly dug ditch outside Madrid where fascists were being shot. "You were telling the truth."

"But in wartime it's not always expedient to tell the truth." He gave me a searching look. "It's troubling, I know. Truth is among the first of war's victims."

He was about to say more when the wail of the air-raid siren sounded. Voices quieted, the room was still except for the undulating siren. The scramble for the exit began. I rose from my seat to find Tom rushing toward me. I murmured a goodbye to Koestler and ran toward Tom. We dashed up the stairs and out onto the street. Our hotel was only half a block away. The planes were not yet overhead, but we could hear the drone of their engines coming closer. Explosions rent the air. Fire lit the horizon and the sky turned red. At the hotel we raced down to the cellar. Residents were crouched against the wall, slumped on chairs. Tom and I found a space on the floor in the corner of the room. A bomb exploded nearby, shaking the walls and the floor beneath us, sending plaster dropping from the ceiling. Tom and I clutched each other. The lights dimmed. A basket of oranges on the bar tipped over and the oranges rolled on the floor. I reached out for one just as another bomb exploded, shaking the building again. More plaster fell. I shivered in Tom's arms and grabbed the orange as it rolled against me.

We spent most of the night on the cold cellar floor, managing to sleep in the lulls between bombings, but the all-clear didn't sound until 4AM. We finally dragged ourselves up the stairs and fell into bed—to be wakened at dawn by artillery fire.

When we returned to the cellar for breakfast, the floors had been swept of plaster and more oranges were piled in the basket on the bar. It had an air of normalcy except for the thundering of artillery fire in the distance. The conversation was about the night's raid, which it was agreed was the Condor Legion. One of the journalists had identified the planes as German Junker 52's escorted by Italian Savoia 81's. The bartender told them he'd heard a radio report that Franco had ordered intensive aerial bombardment of Madrid. Tom speculated that Hitler and Mussolini were experimenting with new weapons and tactics. "Spain is the tryout for the big war they're planning to conquer Europe!"

"Arthur Koestler agrees with you. He said exactly the same thing at dinner last night. Hitler is breaking in his planes and pilots here in Spain."

A haggard Anthony looked up from his cup of coffee. "The bombing raids are supposed to destroy the people's will to the fight."

The bartender lifted his chin. "Well, we'll see about that! Those putas will learn how tough we Madrileños can be."

8
Madrid
November, 1936

Tom rapidly typed the day's story in duplicate, ready for the censor. The boom of artillery fire provided a resonant bass to the staccato tapping of his typewriter keys. In spite of my fear of the Condor Legion, I decided to go with Tom to Barea's office at the Ministry. I had my own piece about Pasionaria and the nuns ready to submit and wanted to learn the procedure. When we stepped out onto the street the smell of plaster dust, gunpowder and smoke made it difficult to breathe. I held my handkerchief over my nose. Black smoke shut out the sunlight. A pile of masonry and pulverized stones on the sidewalk and a bomb crater reaching into the street stopped us. Our hotel had not been hit, but a large section of the upper wall of the building two doors away had fallen, and I could see the remains of bedroom furnishings. A child's broken crib lay on its side next to the open wall. The corner of a tattered white blanket hung over the edge of the building like a flag of surrender.

Two men in yellow jackets were on the street removing rubble from the trolley tracks, which seemed to be intact. A crowd had gathered by the entrance to the building and people were carrying out mattresses and suitcases. Two women were sobbing. I surveyed the street. It was the only structure that had been hit, and fortunately it hadn't caught fire. The construction was of stone, marble and wrought iron, as was the Florida Hotel. A gray-haired, man with a blood stained bandanna tied around his head was carrying a bundle of blankets toward a horse-drawn wagon. In hushed tones Tom asked him if there had been any fatalities.

He stared at Tom with blank eyes. "My two grandsons."

We both mumbled terms of sympathy to the grieving man. I felt an indescribable sense of shock and grief for this family. At the same time, guiltily, I couldn't help but be thankful that it wasn't our building that had been hit. The Junkers would return, of course, and I was tempting fate for thinking such thoughts. I gazed at the wrecked building and the sobbing women. So much destruction and carnage. I then thought of the prisoners in the Model Prison, who hadn't been far from my mind since the evening before. Were more men being shot at this very moment?

We detoured around the debris and walked rapidly to the Junta de Defensa. The artillery had stopped firing, and I could hear the clanging of a trolley bell behind us. The tracks had been cleared already. We entered the Ministry building that housed the Junta and descended to the cellars where the various offices had been arranged in makeshift cubicles. As we threaded our way through the crowd at the bottom of the stairs, I recognized several journalists waiting to see the censor. Ralph Fitzgerald hailed us from across the room, and Koestler tipped his hat to me as he left Barea's office and disappeared in the crowd.

Then I saw an imposing looking man in a long black leather coat and forage cap talking to General Goriev. They were both barging through the crowd, their voices raised. The face of the leather-coated man was twisted in anger. "You promised air support," he shouted, "and rifles! And what did you give me? Antiques!" He marched up the stairs, his black boots stamping on the granite steps. Goriev shrugged and disappeared into one of the cubicles.

When we reached Ralph, he grinned at us. "Do you know who that was?"

"No," said Tom. "Whoever he is he's mad as hell."

"For good reason. That was Buenaventura Durruti, the Anarchist leader. He brought 4,000 of his men from the front in Aragon and late yesterday afternoon began an attack against the Moors. His men refused to go forward. They hadn't experienced machine gun fire and big cannons, and the Junta hadn't provided enough weapons."

"And from what we just heard, he didn't get air support," Tom said.

"Right. And last night the Condor Legion flew in with all their Junker 52's and Savoia 81's and let them have it, poor guys. They've opened up the Ritz hotel as a hospital for the Anarchist troops."

"The Palace for the Communists, the Ritz for the Anarchists," I murmured.

Ralph tugged a pack of Galloises from his shirt pocket and held them out to us. "Yeah, they can't even get together as wounded!"

"Where would they put us if we got hurt in the bombings—with the Communists or the Anarchists?" I asked, attempting a joke.

"Well." He gave a wry smile. "That would be a problem. But seriously, they'd probably take us to the British-American hospital near the British Embassy. That is, if they had room for us. I hear they are harboring refugees."

We then exchanged experiences and observations about the previous night's aerial bombardment. "Maybe, since Varela hasn't been able to take Madrid, Franco has decided to bomb the shit out of it." Tom said to Ralph, moving toward Barea's office. The line of journalists was thinning. Ralph shrugged. The two men then entered the office, and I watched the procedure from the open doorway.

As I waited, I heard raised voices coming from the office next door. I recognized Koltsov's voice. I heard the words *Model Prison* and *Fifth Column*, which hit me with a jolt. Then a furious-faced man stormed out of the office and disappeared into the warren of cubicles. Journalists' heads turned. A French reporter I'd met at the Florida raised his eyebrows and whispered, "alors, yet another outburst from an Anarchist. First Durruiti, now Melchor Rodriguez."

"Who is he?"

"He's just been appointed as governor of prisons. Odd, those Anarchists don't approve of prisons, you know."

I remembered hearing in Barcelona how the Anarchists had emptied the prisons, even of common criminals. Maybe this man would stop the killings. He most certainly was angry. Did he have the power? Unlike the situation in Barcelona, here in Madrid the Communists were in control.

Suddenly, two men in muddy Republican Militia uniforms dashed down the stone stairs, pushed frantically through the crowd and barged into Goriev's office. We all strained our ears to hear what they were saying. In a moment one of Goriev's staff officers rushed into the information office. When he emerged again he held up his hand. He had an important news report. "The column of Moroccans found a gap in the Republican line and made a bridgehead onto this side of the river at University City. They have control of some of the buildings. It's building to building fighting. That's all I know at this moment."

Journalists crowded forward, but the officer returned to Goriev's office refusing to say more. Tom rushed toward me. "Let's get out of here. I need to file my story and then I want to get out to University City. Building to building fighting—that's what Franco wanted to avoid. His Moors do better on open ground. Our Militiamen and Brigaders are city fighters. Maybe it won't be so disastrous."

We hurried up the stairs and walked one block to the Atocha subway station. We didn't know when the next air-raid would begin and Tom needed to get to Telefonica for his broadcast. Two old women were sweeping the floors of the platforms of scraps of newspaper and orange peels. While we waited for the next train, I told Tom about the new prison director, Rodriguez, and his furious exit from Koltsov's office, and how I'd heard them mention the Model Prison. I couldn't say more, since a train then arrived. The car was full and I didn't want to be overheard. We quickly stepped on board and rode the two stops to Puerta del Sol. When we climbed the stairs to the street the air-raid siren was rising and falling in its frightening wail. We managed to run the two blocks to Telefonica before the explosions began, but we could see the fleet of bombers flying toward us. The roar of their engines was terrifying.

Tom took the elevator to the tenth floor, which we both knew could be deadly. The tall building, the telephone exchange, seemed the worst place to be in Madrid at the moment, but Tom insisted he had to make his broadcast. "Go down to the basement!" Tom shouted. "I won't be long! I'll meet you there." The doorman was beckoning me toward the cellar stairs. I descended into the cold lower floor and joined several workers who were taking shelter there. Old wooden desks and chairs had been set up on the cement floor, and office workers had brought down their typewriters or ledger books. I claimed an empty desk in the back of the large space and took my notebook from my pocket and set it in front of me with shaking hands. I thought of Tom on the tenth floor. This important, very visible building would be targeted, and I wondered how accurate the targeting process was. Did the airman in charge of aiming the bomb first peer out the window to the ground below, then judge when he was over the target before he pressed the bomb-release button? Did the pilot press the button?

I examined the cement wall next to me, and the concrete and steel columns that supported the ceiling, and prayed they were well constructed. It was built by American ITT, which should reassure me. At that moment a loud boom sounded and the floor shook beneath me, almost knocking me out of my chair. People around me cried out, a typewriter fell to the floor with a crash. More explosions, three, four, more shaking, more cries of alarm. Clinging to the desk, I lowered myself onto the floor. The bombardment continued it seemed like hours, but was only twenty minutes or so. When the all-clear sounded, I slowly headed for the stairs, accompanied by my white-faced air-raid companions.

I was waiting at the bottom of the stairway to the upper floors when Tom came storming down the steps. We were both alive, unhurt, and had survived yet another bombing raid by the Condor Legion. "They're not finished, you know," Tom said, his arm over my shoulders as we left the building. "They'll be back."

The breath caught in my throat, thinking that I wouldn't be able to take another raid like that one. "Where can we be safe?"

We locked glances. Tom shook his head. "I don't know, but the hotel cellar is as good a place as any. It's a question of luck."

I considered this word *luck* a moment. It didn't reassure me.

Tom peered up at the sky. "I could see those three-engine Junker 52's as they flew above us. The windows upstairs are taped, some are open. There must have been three squadrons of planes flying four abreast. They came over in waves. The little Russian fighters, the Chatos, hit two of the bombers. One went down in the Campo across the river. I didn't see where the other one crashed. The German Heinkel fighters couldn't chase the Chatos away. They were too slow."

"Were you able to broadcast?"

"Amazingly, yes. Along with sound effects from the bombing." His cheeks were flushed and his eyes sparked with excitement. Adrenaline, I supposed. He had to have been scared up there with the bombers flying overhead, but he made his broadcast. I was pretty sure I couldn't have gone through with it. Maybe I wasn't meant to be a war correspondent.

Out on the street we breathed air filled with smoke and gritty dust that I could taste on my tongue. I covered my nose and mouth with my scarf. We could see three buildings on fire. Soldiers of the 5th Regiment were trying to put out the flames with fire hoses. Two blanket-wrapped bodies were being loaded into an ambulance. Numbly, I watched as the orderlies closed the doors.

We hurried down the rubble-strewn Gran Via toward our hotel, which, thank God, hadn't been damaged. At the door, Tom gave me a tight hug. "I'll meet you here in a couple of hours. OK?" I pulled away from him, not knowing what to say. I was scared for him, for myself, and at this moment I wish I'd never come to Spain.

"Meg, I have to go. I have to see for myself how far the Nationalists have penetrated."

"Can't you find out at the press briefing?"

"You can't trust them to tell the truth."

"But how are you going to get out there? The trolleys aren't running."

"I'll take the metro." Then he grinned. "I'll just have to be careful to get off before I'm in Nationalist territory!"

"Oh, Tom," I said, on the verge of tears. "What a war." I tried to smile, but my lips trembled. "It's all crazy."

"You've got that one right. Totally crazy."

We could hear voices and laughter from inside the hotel. "It sounds as though all the reporters aren't out at the front," I said.

"They'll already have filed today's story, I bet. They need a drink— or two or three after that raid."

"I think I'll join them!" I felt tears in my eyes, so gave him a brief wave and went through the door into the atrium.

The Florida's bar was three-deep with reporters. I took a deep breath, resolving to be one of them and moved toward the bar. The bartender was fiddling with the volume on the radio and ordered everyone to shut up! A resonant-voiced woman was speaking. La Pasionaria, of course. "And during the raid keep your windows open. If you go to a shelter, do not block the doorway. Help the elderly down the stairs. And. No Pasarán!" Tinny, martial music then blasted into the room. Immediately, the reporters' raised their voices over the noise of the band and continued their interrupted conversations. Anthony Thomas caught sight of me and called out, "Meg, good to see you! What 'll you have?"

"A brandy, please. And I think I need to sit down." I moved to one of the tables next to the bar and sat on a stud-trimmed red leather chair.

Anthony soon joined me with two glasses of brandy. He folded his thin, tall frame as if it were an umbrella and placed himself on a chair opposite me. "You're looking a bit peckish. Would you like something to eat? I have a few tins of sardines stashed away. Do you fancy some sardines?"

"Anthony, thank you, no. Really, I'm fine, not at all hungry. Just... confused."

"Yeah, who isn't? Is it that bloke of yours?"

"Yes and no. Tom insisted upon going out to University City just now. He wants to check on the report about the Nationalist breakthrough. The new fighting."

"And you didn't want him to go."

"No, I didn't. He could get killed."

Anthony leaned back and peered at me closely. "Tom's a good reporter. Ambitious. Has guts." He reached across the table and patted my hand. "That's his job."

I pulled my hand away, feeling a spurt of anger. "OK, Anthony, I know what you're saying. We Americans have a phrase—if you can't stand the heat get out of the kitchen—don't you think I know that! And what about all of you here at the bar? You're good reporters, aren't you?"

"We've all filed our stories for the day. We have evening papers. Tomorrow is soon enough to get our heads blown off. Tom's a broadcast journalist. Maybe it's different for him. He doesn't have the same kind of deadline."

I stared at him. "I could have gone with him." I felt near tears. "But I'm not brave enough."

Anthony was shaking his head, smiling, his blue eyes filled with sympathy. "Meg, my dear girl, don't expect too much of yourself. This is your first job, your first war, for Christ's sake. Don't fret. Tom will be fine. He knows how to keep his head down."

As Anthony was speaking I could hear that the artillery barrage had started again. I looked at my watch. "It's time for the afternoon shelling,"

Anthony was unfolding himself from the chair. "These Spaniards seem to keep their usual hours even during war. It's 4 o'clock. The siesta is over. And, it's time for the press briefing. Are you coming?"

"I shook my head. "No I was at the office this morning. And by the way, I saw Durruti. He was fuming. Furious with the Russians."

"No air support."

"No. And not enough weapons."

Anthony sighed, saluted, bid me farewell and joined the crowd of reporters leaving the hotel. I listened to the artillery as I slowly sipped my brandy, Glancing around the atrium I saw only one other person. He was sitting at a table by the stairs. He held a newspaper in his hands, but he was looking in my direction. Our glances met. I realized it was Christopher Lance, the engineer we had seen driving the ambulance two nights earlier. He waved, rose to his feet and walked toward me. "Good afternoon. Miss Austin, isn't it?"

"Correct. And you're Christopher Lance."

"Righto. May I join you? And would you like a cup of tea? Or can I get you another drink?"

I smiled. "Tea would be fine." I watched him go to the bar and hand over a packet to the bartender. I wasn't at all sure I wanted to talk to Lance at the moment, but I was curious about him. When he returned to the table I asked him about his driving the ambulance.

He gave me a searching look before he answered. "Miss Austin, I'm going to assume you were telling the truth the other day when you said you were trying to maintain your objectivity about this war."

"I think I need to emphasize the verb try. Personally, I'm against fascism, Hitler, the Nazi's, Franco. But I know my job is to observe and report—not to act for or against one side or the other. I'm also learning that words like truth, good and evil don't mean much during a war."

"But you don't believe in telling lies."

"Certainly not. But I also know that sometimes certain stories can not be told."

"But if I were you to tell you about something I'd witnessed, but asked you never to reveal the source of your information, you would keep that promise."

"Absolutely. I have no trouble at all with that one. It's a rule that has been drummed into me since my first whiff of printers ink at my father's newspaper." As I spoke, I realized my self-confidence as a journalist had returned. He was treating me as a bona fide reporter and I was responding as such.

The waiter had appeared with the tea tray, which he set in front of me, as if I were the English hostess. I poured the tea and sat back in my comfortable chair waiting for Lance to continue. He eyed me over the rim of the teacup. "You're very young, Miss Austin. I hope my story won't be too disturbing to you."

I smiled. "Mr. Lance, please do get on with it. You're a master of suspense." What in the world was this man about to tell me?

"Righto. I'll start at the beginning. Please don't question me until my story is finished."

I set my notebook and pen on the table in front of me. "You have no objection to my taking notes?"

"No. But no names. Agreed?"

"Agreed."

"I suppose you could title this story the Fifth Column."

Those words jolted me into sharp attention. I nodded and he continued. "You wanted to know why I was driving an ambulance. What wounded I was carrying to the hospital. Well, I wasn't carrying wounded. I was taking a former prisoner from the Model Prison to the British-American hospital. The man was a scientist, strictly apolitical. He had no business being arrested. Certainly, he ought not to be shot by the Communists. I had use of the ambulance because I had already driven a few of my countrymen to the port at Alicante where they boarded a ship returning to England. They were ill and had needed special care."

I started to speak, wanting to ask how he knew the man would be shot, but Lance held up his hand. "Let me tell my story. Soon after General Mola made his unfortunate remark about the Fifth Column, my friend who runs the British American hospital, Mary Sutherland, called me to say that several frightened Madrileños had taken shelter there. Since the British Embassy had moved to Valencia people thought of the hospital as the Embassy's extension."

I nodded. I had heard the rumors. I had assumed the Russians knew also but didn't want to provoke the British and had left the hospital in peace.

Lance continued. "Mary knew the Ambassador had appointed me as temporary attaché. She then asked me to call on two young ladies of a well-to-do family who were frantically worried about their young brother, who had been arrested by the Seguridad. I went to visit them in their elegant apartment in the Salamanca district. They were lovely girls. Their brother, Manuel, was only sixteen and they had not heard from him since the day he was arrested. They asked me for help."

He picked up his teacup, drank a little, set it down again, pausing in his tale as if to marshal his thoughts. "Well, you can imagine, Miss Austin, how puzzled I was about what to do. The Seguridad is nothing to fool with. I finally decided to go directly to the prison. I confronted the governor, an unpleasant man, by the way, demanding to know the whereabouts of Manuel. The governor showed me papers that indicated the boy had been released the previous day. I returned to the young ladies' apartment to tell them what I had learned. While I was there an old man arrived at their door from Paracuellos de Jarama to tell the girls he thought he had seen their brother being led away with other prisoners."

At the words *Paracuellos de Jarama* I knew where this story would lead. I bit my lip to keep myself from asking him to stop and stared into my teacup.

Lance shifted in his chair. He frowned. "The girls were upset of course and asked me if it was possible for me to go to that village to see what I could find out. It's only a few kilometers outside Madrid, and as a civil engineer I have papers to travel in that area. My car was marked with the Union Jack and I wore a British brassard on my arm. I had no trouble at the roadblocks. I parked the car in front of the village church and asked a man, a local peasant, if he had seen prisoners there. He told me he had, indeed, and would show me where they were. He took me to a chickpea field outside the village and showed me a long, low mound. I didn't want to believe what the mound contained." Lance paused and fixed his blue eyes on mine as if he were checking on how I was reacting to his story.

"Go on," I murmured.

In a low, hoarse voice he continued. "I asked the man if the prisoners were buried there and he said 'oh yes, I helped dig the grave.' How deep is it? I asked. 'Not very,' he said. 'We had to dig it in a hurry. They're piled in three deep.' I paced the length of the mound and calculated that there must be forty bodies buried there. I then described Manuel and asked the old man if he had seen someone who looked like him. He said that he had, that he noticed the boy because he was so young and dressed in expensive clothes as if he came from a wealthy family."

Lance spooned more sugar into his tea, stirred it rapidly then sipped it slowly. I thought of English officers in the Great War and their reputation of calling for tea at four o'clock in the midst of trench warfare. "And then you had to go to the boy's sisters to tell them the tragic news." I said slowly, feeling on the edge of nausea.

"Yes." He set down his teacup. "It was a terrible scene. And I was so angry, so terribly angry. I went back to that burial spot before daybreak the next day. It was very cold and still dark. Twenty-five bloodied corpses, one a middle-aged woman, lay at the side of the road. They had multiple wounds at breast height, obviously done by a machine gun. Then they'd been given a final pistol shot to the head. To make sure they were dead. The *coup de grace.*"

We both remained silent for a few moments. I poured him more tea and filled up my cup, the lid of the teapot rattling in my hand. I would have preferred another shot of brandy. "Mr. Lance," I said, "just what do you want me to do with this story? You know the censors would never let it be published—or broadcast—and I'm not sure I'd want another Republican atrocity documented for the use of their enemies' propaganda machine."

He gave me a long look before he answered. "I know, Miss Austin. I also know you won't be here in Spain forever. The war will end. You will go home. Then you can tell the truth."

"But this is something you can do yourself."

"That may not be possible. I have set myself a task. I want to help these innocent people survive. To make a long story short, I discovered that when a prisoner's release is announced it means he or she will be taken away to be shot. I have found a way to collect these prisoners the day they are supposed to be released."

"And you take them to the British hospital in an ambulance. And then you transport them to Alicante where they can escape the country by ship."

"That's all I want to say at the moment."

I thought of the scene at the Junta de Defensa this morning when I saw Melchor Rodriguez rushing away in anger. I described it to Lance. "I believe Rodriguez, an Anarchist, will put a stop to the shootings."

"We shall see." Lance rose from his chair and gave me a polite bow. "Thank you, Miss Austin, for listening." He turned smartly, cinched the belt of his raincoat and left the hotel. As I watched the doors swing shut behind him, I speculated that Lance was about to attempt to rescue as many rich people of Madrid as he could. He'd probably take them by ambulance to Alicante—along with the British who were desperate to leave Spain. A perilous mission.

For several minutes after Lance left, I barely moved. His story had left me stunned and disheartened. If the Anarchist guard at the Model Prison hadn't told us the prisoners where being killed, I would not have believed Lance. I didn't want to know that these Communists murdered innocent people. La Pasionaria had been so generous in her praise of Russian Communists, I had wanted to believe in their integrity. At the same time, I had heard the metal in Koltsov's voice when he said that the Fifth Columnists must be eliminated.

Finally, I rose from my chair and took refuge in my room. I immediately opened my Corona portable and began to write about my visit to the hospital the day before. I didn't want to think about Communist atrocities. Instead I wrote about the passion and bravery of the Militia fighters and the men of the International Brigade. I would send this story and the one about La Pasionaria's nuns to my father, who had written to me saying he had a friend who was an editor at Colliers who might publish my pieces.

Before I had finished a second paragraph, Tom burst into the room. He was out of breath but was uninjured, thank God. He bounded toward me and hugged me as I sat at my typewriter. He glanced at my page. "Ah, you're doing a piece about the hospital. Great!"

"So, Tom, was the report true? Are the Nationalists fighting on this side of the river?"

"Indeed they are. The Moroccans have taken the School of Architecture building. Durruti's men are firing their old rifles from the school of Philosophy. The soldiers of the Thaelmann Brigade are on the lower floors of the Clinic. They're putting explosives on the elevators to explode on the upper floors where some Moroccans are holed up. Bizarre! I was glad to get out of there. The metro is still running from the University City stop, thank God."

Tom was filled with energy and excitement. I wanted to tell him about Lance. I watched as he flung off his coat, draped it over a chair and fished out his Luckies. He held out the almost empty pack to me. I took one and he lit it, then his own. I shoved my Corona back on the table and reached for my notebook. Flipping the pages to the notes I had taken of Lance's story, I looked up at Tom. "I had a long talk with Christopher Lance this afternoon."

"Lance? The British engineer? Did he tell you what he was doing driving the ambulance yesterday?"

"He did. And more. Much more."

Tom pulled up a chair and sat opposite me at the small table. "From the look in your eyes I would guess that what he told you was unpleasant."

"It was, indeed. He began by telling me to title the story the Fifth Column."

Tom gave me a searching look. "And what did he mean?"

I took a deep breath and repeated what Lance had told me about the sixteen-year old boy and the shooting of prisoners. Tom didn't interrupt me and when I was finished he jumped up from his chair. "Jesus Christ, what a story—from two sources. And we can't do a damned thing with it. We'd never persuade the democracies to send arms to the Republicans if any inkling of that story got out."

"I know. There's nothing we can do. I hope this new prison governor can protect the prisoners. But those Russians! They're so paranoid."

"Have you thought that they might be right."

"Right? Are you kidding? Killing innocent sixteen year old boys?"

"No, I'm serious. How do you know that sixteen year old is innocent?

He may be part of the fascist plot. Maybe the Fifth Column really exists. "

I gazed at Tom in astonishment. "Tom, you're siding with the Russians, making excuses for their crimes." Had I made a mistake in confiding in him? I hadn't told Tom my speculations about Lance's plans. How Lance hadn't denied my question about his helping upper class Madrileños escape to Alicante. "Tom, you know I gave my solemn promise to Lance I wouldn't divulge the source of the story."

Tom reached across the table and took hold of my hand. "Don't worry. You can trust me. Personally, I may side with the Republic—and the Communists, but I'm also a journalist. It's a tricky tightrope we walk."

"Indeed." I withdrew my hand and went to the window, where I pulled the blackout curtains closed. It was almost dark and soon the air-raid siren would sound. I was feeling uneasy about having told Tom what Lance had witnessed. I had given Lance my promise not to reveal his name. Could I truly trust Tom? Could I trust him not to leak to Koltsov that Lance had been to the site of the shootings? Was Tom more of a Stalinist than I thought? At least I hadn't mentioned my speculations about Lance's plans to help Madrileños escape to Alicante. If Tom asked me about what he was doing driving the ambulance I'd tell him he was taking some English women to the British hospital. I turned and glanced at Tom, who was pouring over his notes. This was the first time since I had known Tom that I wanted to keep something from him, and I didn't feel good about it. I felt uneasy, uncertain.

That evening our meal, such as it was, was interrupted once more by the air-raid siren. Again we spent most of the night in the hotel cellar, shivering with cold and fright, although this time we had brought pillows and blankets. Again, glassware, coffee cups, and plaster from the ceiling fell crashing to the cement floor. We crawled under a table, covered ourselves with blankets and dozed in between explosions. My fear of the bombing was stronger than my disappointment in Tom and I found myself huddling close to him. I would consider his political leanings some other time.

The next two days and nights, the Condor Legion and the artillery kept up an almost continuous bombardment. We spent most of our time either in the hotel cellar or the underground. Tom made two dashes across the street in between aerial bombardments to broadcast his stories from Telefonica. Fortunately, he'd already obtained Barea's stamp of approval. I searched for open food stores along the pockmarked streets and ruined buildings. I also photographed the ruined buildings.

On one of my frantic excursions outside the safety of the cellar, the artillery fire started up again. The shells were flying high over my head aimed at Telefonica. A woman and a small boy, perhaps four years old, were running almost at my side. An explosion shook the pavement. The woman screamed. The little boy crumpled onto the stone sidewalk, a piece of shrapnel piercing his skull. The woman lifted him into her arms, blood dripping onto her coat, smearing her face as she held the child close. I rushed to her side, felt the boy's bloodied throat for a pulse, but there was nothing I could do. He was dead. The woman looked up at the sky, screaming with anger. Another two women ran toward the grieving mother and led her and the dead child away.

I stood at that spot, numb, unable to move, until another shell exploded nearby. I ran back to my hotel room where I washed the child's blood from my hands in the bathroom sink. I didn't cry. I cursed Franco and Hitler's German pilots and felt bursting with hatred at the fascist monsters, at the rich landholders and aristocrats for supporting the generals. I continued to run water into the basin and watched it turn pink, then run clear. I turned off the faucet, dried my hands on a white towel, and stared into the mirror. I didn't recognize the person who stared back at me.

The next day, the 29th of November, the air-raid sirens didn't wail. That night we went to bed almost fully dressed expecting to be awakened. At first I had difficulty erasing the image of the dead boy and his mother from my mind, her head thrown back, screaming at the sky, but I was too exhausted to remain awake long. I also had stored away my frisson of distrust of Tom. I would consider it later when I was less exhausted. My overriding feeling that night was anger. Hatred of Franco and his German and Italian pilots and his artillery guns seeped through my veins like snake venom.

I awoke at dawn, amazed. We had slept the entire night. Tom lay next to me sound asleep. I fixed my sleep-blurred eyes on his untidy blond hair and the stubble on his chin. I loved him, I knew, even if I didn't agree with his allegiance to the Stalinists, but there had been a shift in my feelings toward him.

As I considered this new feeling, a shaft of sunlight fell across his face. He awoke with a start. "My God, it's morning," he murmured. "Meg, we've slept all night! No planes? No bombs?" He reached for me and I quickly forgot my doubts. We began to make love, removing our clothes piece by piece. We were young and alive and the sun was shining—and the bombing had stopped—for the moment.

At breakfast that morning, which consisted of half a stale bread roll and one cup of watery coffee, we heard on the radio that Franco had met with his generals and decided to end the attack on Madrid. We knew that during the two previous days the Moroccans had advanced as far as the Model Prison on the Plaza de Moncloa. They had been pushed back three times and had lost huge numbers of their men. Madrileños, Anarchists and the International Brigades had fought bravely and fiercely. Many died. As Pasionaria had preached, they did not allow the enemy to pass. Franco was forced to stop his assault on Madrid.

When Tom first told me about the battle in front of the Model Prison I thought of the time a few nights before when we were at that very place, listening to the Anarchist guard whisper his story of the shooting of prisoners. What had happened to the prisoners who remained? Had Rodriguez moved them to safety? I hadn't seen Lance since the afternoon we spoke, and Tom hadn't asked about our seeing him drive the ambulance. I wondered if Lance had helped more Fifth Column suspects escape Communist arrests. It was strange for me to feel I could not discuss Lance with Tom, but I still felt I couldn't trust him not to leak Lance's name to Koltsov. Anyway, Tom was too busy ferreting out the news of the battle at the Model Prison.

So what would happen now? I would no longer need to be afraid that the dread Moors would come storming into our hotel. The battle would no longer be a mere mile away from our hotel, although artillery shells still whistled over our heads. Whenever I was out on the street I thought of the boy with shrapnel piercing his skull. I could still feel the sticky blood on my hand.

The big guns were still in place on the hill above the Casa de Campo aimed at Telefonica. The upper three floors had been hit and were closed, but the building was sturdy. Our hotel stood between the guns and the telephone building—like a tennis net marking two courts. The eastern wall of the hotel had been hit at least three times so far, but sustained little damage. The whistling was blood chilling when the shells whizzed over us. We could see the explosions west of us from our open windows and smell the smoke. The grit of granite and ash coated our tongues and caught in our throats.

The first day after Franco's withdrawal brought us out on the streets to survey the damage. Craters where bombs had fallen were scattered on walkways, streets and plazas. Some buildings looked like honeycombs or doll houses without external walls, furniture still in place. Others were completely destroyed. I watched as a gray-haired woman tugged a framed photograph of a bride and groom out from under the rubble, it's glass shattered. Streetcar tracks were twisted and broken, but men were already repairing them. On the sidewalk near our hotel I saw a trail of blackened blood leading to an underground shelter.

It wasn't yet known how many Madrid civilians had been killed in the raids. The numbers of men slain at the front also had not yet been counted, but we knew it would number in the thousands. The people of Madrid had fought with passion. The bombing of their city had increased their resolve to fight Franco and his Moors and Germans and Italians.

That first evening free of air-raids Tom and I decided to go to Gaylord's to glean the latest news from the Russians. I also wanted to see Pasionaria. I had translated my story written about her and the nuns into Spanish for her to read. I hoped for her approval before I sent it to my father.

Gaylord's was crowded and the air was thick with cigarette smoke. The table in the center of the large room was loaded with bottles of vodka and platters of canapés. "We're in luck, Tom," I said. "Food! How do they do it!" We edged our way closer to the table.

Tom shrugged. "Ours not to wonder why…" He grinned and whispered, "maybe they load up their tanks and planes with vodka instead of gasoline."

I wanted to say something about the Spanish gold that paid for the vodka and caviar, but this was not the time or place. Koltsov was approaching us. "Ah, Margarita, Tomás, you've come to celebrate

Franco's defeat." He splashed vodka into glasses and handed them to us. "Salud!" he said, holding up his glass .

"And victory," Tom added.

A waiter then offered us canapés of caviar, egg and onions on thin pieces of toast, which we quickly devoured. My stomach growled with pleasure. I hadn't eaten much the last two days. The Gran Via had been closed, and our diet had consisted of oranges, dry bread and sardines. Tom had traded two precious packs of cigarettes for two cans of sardines. He now had only one carton of Luckies remaining.

Across the room I spied Pasionaria speaking to Orlov. Their heads were close together as if they were locked in a secret exchange of information. I hesitated to interrupt them. I snatched up another canapé and moved slowly in their direction. A man I didn't know approached Orlov and whispered in his ear. Orlov then bowed to Pasionaria and walked briskly with the man toward the exit.

Pasionaria greeted me warmly. We spoke in Spanish, of course. I told her about my story, fished the manuscript from my bag and handed it to her. She promised to read it that evening.

"And, Dolores, I want to congratulate you."

"Me?"

"Yes, your broadcasts to the people of Madrid, your repeated *no pasarán*, spurred them on to action, strengthened their resolve to fight."

Pasionaria shook her head. "The working people of Madrid have hearts like lions. I had little to do with it." She frowned. "And now it's imperative the various militias join together as the Popular Front army. Unfortunately, the militias don't always want to engage the enemy on other territory but their own. They must fight where they're ordered to fight. As Comrade Stalin says, discipline is essential."

"I suppose it's natural for men to want to guard their own homes."

"Yes, but they must learn to see the broader view. They must fight for all Spain against fascism. We will attach a political commissar to each battalion to educate the soldiers, to enlighten them, to help them understand why they're fighting."

"A political commissar?" I had heard about this practice in Russia, and had felt sympathy for the people who had to listen to the Communist catechism. I couldn't imagine battle-stained soldiers listening to doctrine spouted by commissars. From what I'd heard, the Party line was dictated by Stalin and changed when it was expedient to do so. Pasionaria worshiped Stalin. I wanted to maintain my friendly relationship with her. I would need to be circumspect.

"Yes. And we must also rid the ranks of charlatánes y traidores." Her words echoed those of Koltsov's when he spoke of eliminating the Fifth Columnist traitors. I immediately felt apprehensive. She reached into her shoulder bag and pulled out a newspaper cutting. "I want you to read this. It's a piece recently published in the POUM newspaper, La Batalla."

I unfolded the cutting, translating as I read: *Stalin's concern is not really the fate of the Spanish and international proletariat, but the protection of the Soviet government in accordance with the policy of pacts made by certain others.* The words were simple enough. I didn't have any doubts about my translation.

Pasionaria watched me read, her raptor eyes hard as stone. "The POUMistas have sold out to international fascism. Comrade Orlov has just informed me that pay and supplies would be cut off from these Trotskyistas charlatánes on the Madrid front."

So, I thought, there would be a witch-hunt like the one that was happening in the Soviet Union. The struggle between the two Marxist groups had spilled over into Spain. It seemed to me the article spoke the truth. Since Stalin's pact with France he had put aside the goal of international revolution, which Trotsky still championed. Stalin was appeasing the Western democracies.

I returned the clipping to Pasionaria. "I didn't realize POUM had a militia fighting here in Madrid. I thought most were in Catalonia or in Aragon."

"It's a small militia, but could be dangerous. They're not to be trusted."

As she spoke I was relieved to see Tom come toward me. I hadn't known how to respond to Pasionaria. I didn't want to offend her, but I felt certain that it would be disastrous for the anti-fascist organizations to fight each other. I decided to hold my tongue. Pasionaria was my most important source. It would be expedient for me to keep my mouth shut, to keep my views to myself. I was learning my craft.

Part II

9
Madrid
1937

If I had believed that Franco's inability to capture Madrid would lead to the end of danger, I was mistaken. The three weeks of aerial bombardment had ceased, but the artillery shelling continued: before breakfast, before lunch and late afternoon. Telefonica was now the major target of the big guns that stood on a hilltop two miles away. The building still remained standing, but many of the structures around it were in ruins. By the time the assault on Madrid ended I had been in Spain less than one month. It seemed much, much longer, an eternity. In those three weeks I had become a seasoned correspondent. I felt older but not wiser. In fact, as the political realities unfolded, I felt confused, less certain, more ignorant than ever. There was so much I didn't understand.

And the war continued. Now Franco attempted to encircle the city, attacking the roads to Valencia, Guadalajara, and San Lorenzo del Escorial. Madrid's POUM militia was dissolved and its soldiers either disappeared or joined the Anarchist or Socialist militias. Rumors circulated about the Stalinists' persecution of the Trotskyists. La Pasionaria spoke of them as traitors, enemies of the people, as fascist spies. The Moscow trials continued and we heard reports of the execution of followers of Trotsky or other *traitors*. Tom made excuses for the Communists. "Maybe these Trotskyists *are* traitors. How do we know they're not fascist spies?" he said, one evening after a visit to Gaylord's. I no longer argued with him. It was obvious Tom had become a true believer, and I had no evidence to counter his beliefs. "We live in terrible times," he said, "and sometimes we have to do terrible things."

I noted the *we* but didn't respond. I thought of Lance. I had seen him only once since he told me of the macabre scene he uncovered in Paracuellos de Jarama. I was hurrying along one of the narrow back streets on my way to the Ministry between artillery bombardments when I saw him. He was wearing the brassard of the British embassy on the sleeve of his tweed coat. He was a few feet in front of me and I called out to him. Was he still rescuing well-to-do Madrileños, I wondered? He stopped, took a quick look behind him. When he recognized me he smiled and waited for me to catch up. We shook hands and engaged in the usual exchange of information about the bombardment. We then walked briskly along the quiet, winding street together. I asked him if he knew about the fate of the prisoners since Rodriguez had become governor of the prisons. "Miss Austin, Rodriguez is humane. He's stopped the killings of his prisoners, but..." He stopped, glanced around, then in a low voice said, "but Orlov and his spies have opened secret prisons—in Madrid and Valencia. The torture and killing goes on."

I stared at him. "How do you know? Who are your sources?"

"I can't tell you, but I heard it from someone who survived the torture and remained alive after he was tossed in a ditch."

"Where are they, these secret prisons?"

"I don't know exact locations. My source had been blindfolded, but when I find out, I'll try to let you know." We had arrived at the Plaza Mayor, which had survived the bombing almost unscathed. Workmen were repairing a crater in the middle of the square, but the buildings had not been damaged. "But now I must go," Lance said. We shook hands, said our farewells, and he crossed to the opposite side of the square. I watched as he disappeared into one of the graceful old buildings of pink stone and lacy wrought iron balconies. I had mixed feelings about Lance. He was a brave man, but could be pro-Franco—most certainly anti-Communist. Was he telling the truth? Did the secret prisons exist? And was it true that Orlov's agents tortured and killed suspected fascist spies?

In the meantime the war went on. Besides Franco's attempt to encircle Madrid, the Nationalists were active in other parts of the country. They fought Republican troops in Aragon and captured Málaga. Reporters who had covered those battles and who found their way back to Madrid told us of the thousands of civilians killed in the bombings. Anyone suspected of being on the side of the Republic was arrested and executed. Ralph Fitzgerald, had gone with my friend, Arthur Koestler, to cover the war in Málaga before the Nationalists attacked in full force. Fitzgerald and two other journalists who had traveled with him left the town when they realized the Nationalists were about to win the battle. "Koestler didn't leave with us. He stayed behind with his friend, the British Consul. He thought he would be safe, but God knows what will happen to him."

I thought about what Koestler had told me about his experience in Seville when he escaped to Gibralter hours before he was to be arrested as a spy. Why would he take such a chance? Was getting a story more important than being safe, staying alive? I knew if it had been me I would have fled. The more I heard about how reckless many of these war correspondents were the more I knew I didn't want to cover battles. What I had found important to write about was on the home front, behind the lines.

While Tom covered the fighting on the outskirts of Madrid, I stood in line with the heroic but distraught Madrileñas at bakeries and food shops, attempting to supplement the Gran Via's meager fare. I listened to the women's stories of their shelled houses or their relatives killed or wounded. Their faces expressed pain, but their spines were made of steel. *No pasarán* was their refrain. When the shelling got bad I returned to my room and wrote about what I'd heard. I also visited hospitals and talked to wounded men from the International Brigades. Americans in the Abraham Lincoln Brigade were now fighting outside Madrid. I sometimes wrote letters for the ones whose wounds would prevent them from writing themselves.

If I were out on the street when the shelling began, I thought of the little boy with the shrapnel sticking out of his skull. Although many more were killed in the bombardment, and I had seen crushed and bloodied dead bodies lying on the street or being carried away, I witnessed only one more death in those weeks after the attempt to capture Madrid ended. One afternoon as I was hurrying back to the hotel, I heard the shell whistling over my head and then an explosion.

A woman ten feet in front of me suddenly collapsed onto the pavement. I ran to her side, but the back of her head was a mass of blood and oozing brains. She had been hit by shrapnel and was quite dead. Two men hurried to her side and carried her body away. I numbly stared at the smear of blood on the pavement and then hearing another whistling shell, I raced toward the hotel and ran up the stairs to my room. I was breathing in gasps. How could anyone be enamored of war? How I hated Franco.

That evening when Tom returned from covering the battle on Corunna Road just outside Madrid, I described what I had witnessed that afternoon. "It was so sudden, so unexpected. Of course I know people get killed during the shelling. I know those shells could hit me, but I don't believe it will happen. Then reality hits—like the woman today—and I'm terrified. And filled with anger at Franco—and the Germans and Italians."

Tom stamped out his cigarette in the ashtray. "And the Brits, the French and our fellow Americans for allowing it to happen. They're the ones I'm furious with. They could have stopped Franco. They could have sent guns and planes. It could have been over by now. France and Britain will be next!"

I fixed my eyes on his. "And the nightmare will go on."

The fighting in the towns encircling Madrid was fierce. Republican casualties at the battle of the Corunna Road had reached 15,000 by the time it ended in a stalemate. Tom was in the field a great deal of the time—along with many other celebrated journalists. Sometime he would be gone three or four days. I worried about him, but didn't allow myself to dwell on it. I was becoming tougher, putting some distance between us. I drank wine with the boys.

Tom's Spanish had improved considerably, and he no longer needed me as interpreter. He suggested that while he was at the front, I should take over the broadcasting chore. When I first heard his suggestion I was both pleased and afraid—pleased that Tom thought I was up to the task—and afraid I'd freeze in front of the microphone. I didn't believe that the bureau chief would agree to a greenhorn like me doing the broadcast. Tom sent him one of my pieces about the wounded soldiers in the Palace Hotel, and much to my surprise and trepidation he gave his approval. When Tom was in the field, I broadcast five-minute feature pieces. I used material from articles I'd written about Pasionaria, the nuns, the hospital and women I'd talked to on the street. My most difficult broadcast was the one of the boy being hit by shrapnel.

I suffered severe stage fright during my first broadcast. Fortunately, it was between artillery bombardments. In those three months after Franco stopped the big assault on Madrid I made five broadcasts. Two were in the midst of artillery bombardments. On those two terrifying occasions, I dashed across the street to Telefonica and took the elevator to the tenth floor. The top three floors were badly shelled and were closed. From the windows I could see the flash of the guns firing. Then after a few seconds hear the detonation of the shell. I was numb with fear, a fear quite unlike stage fright. The censor, whose fingernails were bitten to the quick, prized the duplicate copy of my story from my clenched fingers and led me into the broadcasting booth. I took several deep breaths and forced myself to concentrate on my script and the microphone. The moment I was off-mike, I raced down the stairs to the cellar where I stayed until the shelling stopped.

In March Tom was back doing a daily report. Madrileños had something to celebrate. Republican troops had prevented the encirclement of Madrid. They had defeated the Nationalists in Guadalajara. The shelling of Madrid continued, however. Surprisingly, the shelling did nothing to stop the influx of celebrities housed at the Florida. Most of these celebrities were unknown to me, but in March when Ernest Hemingway burst into the hotel doors and entered the atrium I knew exactly who he was. I'd seen his photographs, of course, his muscular arms holding up a huge blue marlin or steering his yacht. I had read everything of his and considered his clear, uncluttered style astonishing. I worshiped him. Another writer I admired arrived a day later, John Dos Passos. Then Martha Gellhorn turned up. I didn't know who she was, but Tom informed me she was a freelance journalist and had been seen with Hemingway. She wasn't much older than I—five years or so—and had reddish-blonde hair and long, shapely legs, which she seemed to know how to show off. We did not become friends. I was more than a little in awe of her. Not only was she Hemingway's girlfriend, she was said to be a close friend of Eleanor Roosevelt, whom I worshiped.

Hemingway was covering the Civil War for the North American Newspaper Alliance (NANA), and Dos Passos had come to work on a documentary movie, *The Spanish Earth,* with the leftist Dutch filmmaker, Joris Ivens. Leftist intellectuals in the U.S. had raised money to make the film. Ivens was also staying at the Florida. Dos Passos was famous for his book *Manhattan Transfer* and his recently published *The Big Money.* I remembered seeing his face on the cover of Time Magazine a month or so before we left for Spain.

It soon became obvious to most of us at the hotel that Gellhorn and Hemingway were having an affair. We all knew he was still married to his second wife, Pauline. Hemingway's private life was a frequent subject for columnists and magazine hacks gossip—and of the reporters in Madrid.

The Florida became livelier than ever after Hemingway arrived. When the shells were screaming over our hotel roof, he would open the windows and door to his room, put a Chopin mazurka on his Victrola and share his seemingly inexhaustible supply of whiskey. Tom and I were not in his select circle of celebrities, but he knew who we were. He'd often lean over the atrium balcony in the morning and call out to us offering ham and eggs. He kept a supply of food in his suite which his protegé, the sandy-haired American bullfighter, Sidney Franklin, cooked on a camp stove. The aroma of frying ham floated down to the atrium floor from his open door.

Hemingway and Dos Passos were often together, drinking, joking, arguing. They had been friends for years and were now collaborating on the film with Ivers. Dos Passos was known as a leftist. I wasn't sure what Hemingway's politics were, but he loved Spain and the Spanish people, which was obvious to anyone reading *The Sun Also Rises.* He was a powerful presence in Madrid. There was a kind of magnificence about his black beard, bulky six-foot figure and commanding voice. Tom admired him for his bravery, his sense of adventure. It seemed strange to me that after writing a pacifist novel like *A Farewell to Arms* that Hemingway would be so enamored of war.

Tom and I continued to go to Gaylord's for the latest news—and the caviar. Hemingway and his entourage were also frequent visitors. I noticed that he and Koltsov seemed to be good friends. Koltsov could be charming and his English was impeccable. Although I appreciated his intelligence and wit, I also could not forget the steel in his voice when he spoke of eliminating Fifth Columnists.

It was at Gaylords that I was introduced to Dos Passos—by Pasionaria. When I entered the room I saw the two of them in earnest conversation. Dolores saw me and called me over. She and Dos Passos were speaking Spanish. "Here is another rare American who speaks our language," she said, smiling. "Another writer. She's with NBC radio. And now you must excuse me." She wandered off into the crowd.

I was struck dumb for a few moments. I sipped my vodka, utterly incapable of speaking to this great novelist. Fortunately, he spoke first. "And where did you learn your Spanish?" he asked in English. His smile was gentle, almost sad, and when he peered at me through his thick glasses it seemed to me he really was listening to what I would say. He was wearing a gray tweed jacket over a brown sweater and his tall, thin form moved awkwardly. His appearance wasn't at all intimidating.

I told him about Caridad, our Mexican housekeeper, and then asked him about his Spanish. He spoke with the accent of Castile, not of Latin America as I did.

"When I graduated from college in 1916 I came to Madrid to do post-graduate studies in art and architecture. I spent a year here and learned the language."

"What a wonderful place to study art. Unfortunately, I haven't been able to see the El Grecos in Toledo—or even the Goyas and Velasquez here in Madrid. Toledo was in Nationalist hands when I got here and the Prado paintings had been stored in the cellars."

"Unfortunate, indeed." In an instant his smile disappeared, and in a low voice asked, "and just when did you arrive here, Miss Austin."

"Please, call me Margarita like Pasionaria does."

"Fine, Margarita it will be, and you must call me Dos."

I felt myself blushing. I couldn't believe I was on first-name basis with this famous writer. He was so much friendlier than the other celebrities in Hemingway's coterie, for whom I was invisible. "I arrived the beginning of November, just as the big assault on Madrid began."

"Then you've been tried by fire, Margarita," and he leaned forward, speaking quietly. "Did you come here to Gaylords then? Or to the Ministry?"

I gave him a direct look. "Yes, my colleague, Tom Wells and I came for news—and the Ministry for censorship of our stories. In between bombings, of course. Why do you ask?"

"Tell me, did by any chance you meet a Spaniard called José Robles? He's a colonel in the Republican army and an aide to General Goriev. He was here in Madrid during Franco's assault. He speaks Russian as well as American English. He lived in the States for several years and was a professor at Johns Hopkins University. You may have noted his American accent."

"Robles? No, I don't remember anyone of that name. What does he look like?"

"Tall, muscular, dark—and very Spanish-looking. Narrow face, straight nose, expressive dark eyes. He comes from an aristocratic family, but broke with it because of his leftist views. He was on a vacation with his wife and children when the insurgency began. He decided to stay."

Dos Passos' expression was shadowed. He looked troubled. I forced myself to recall men I had seen here. "It's difficult to say. This place is generally packed with Spaniards and Russians. Many are multi-lingual."

Dos Passos sighed. "José's a good friend of mine. I met him here in Spain the year I was studying art. He showed me the old Spain, including bullfights and flamenco. And we remained friends in the States. But now he seems to have disappeared."

"Disappeared?" That word made me uneasy, immediately bringing to mind Lance's tales of executed prisoners and secret prisons.

Dos Passos hesitated. He lowered his voice again. "Actually, he was arrested in Valencia, abruptly taken from his apartment by unknown men. I've been trying to find out what happened to him. People here clam up when I mention his name."

I didn't know how to respond. I glanced behind me to see who could hear what we were saying. Why was famous John Dos Passos telling me, a nobody, all this? "I'm sorry, sir. Believe me, if I had heard anything I'd tell you. Rumors do circulate amongst the press corps, but I've heard nothing about your friend."

Over Dos' shoulder I saw Tom approaching. I introduced him to Dos Passos. Shaking his hand, Tom asked, "I understand you're working on a film about the war here."

"Dos Passos nodded. "Yes, Hem and I are working on the script.

Ivens is the director and photographer. But now you must excuse me. And, Margarita, if you hear anything…"

He turned, and with stooped shoulders, walked slowly through the crowd to the circle of people surrounding Hemingway. I glanced at Tom, deciding not to repeat what Dos Passos had told me, but knowing he would ask. "So, Tom, let's go to Chicotes."

10
Madrid
April, 1937

The day after my puzzling conversation with Dos Passos about his
friend, José Robles, I received a note from Pasionaria. It was a request
that I attend a fiesta at the Duke of Tovar's castle outside Madrid. The
affair was to celebrate the transfer of command of the 15th International
Brigade to the Republic. The Brigade would now be part of the Popular
Army. She hoped I would ride to the celebration with her and Josephine
Herbst, an American writer. I knew that the 15th Brigade was made
up of North Americans—the battalions Abraham Lincoln, George
Washington, and Canada's Mackenzie-Papeneau. I immediately
answered Pasionaria's note agreeing to her request. I soon discovered
that almost all Hotel Florida residents would be at the fiesta, including
Hemingway, Dos Passos, Gellhorn and the entire press corps. Tom
would ride with the boys.

I had not read Herbst's novels, but I had read her article in *The Nation*
earlier in the year. She had expressed her alarm at Hitler's suppression
of labor unions and persecution of Marxists—and his permitting the
concentration of wealth to be in the hands of the big industrialists. She
was obviously a Marxist and most certainly anti-fascist. I also knew she
had been in Paris the same time as Hemingway and Dos Passos in the
twenties. She would be about the same age as they were, around forty.

The morning of the celebration, much to our alarm, we were all
awakened at dawn by a shell crashing into the hotel. The explosion

shook us out of bed. Almost immediately another shrieking shell came nearer and then was silent. Then BOOM, another hit.

"Good God," Tom shouted. "They're aiming at the Florida. They're not just missing Telefonica!" More explosions, more sounds of broken windows, falling plaster, and high-pitched voices of frightened guests catapulted us into action. We threw on our clothes and rushed out onto the balcony overlooking the atrium. Crowds of partially dressed people streamed out of open doors and rushed toward our side of the hotel, away from the shelling. A slight, middle-aged woman clutching a navy-blue robe close to her throat stood in front of the room next to me. She pressed herself against the wall, as if distancing herself as much as she could from the explosions. Then I spied Dos Passos. He stopped beside the woman in the blue robe and placed his hand on her shoulder. "Josie," he said, "are you OK?"

The woman nodded, but didn't speak. When another shell detonated across from us, "Jesus!" she cried faintly. "Are we being bombed?"

It was then that Dos Passos recognized me. "Margarita," he called out. "Does this happen often? This shelling?"

"No," I said, breathing rapidly, moving toward him. "We've had a hit once in a while when they've missed Telefonica, but this is the first time we've been the target."

Tom, who was at my side, gave Dos Passos a reassuring look. "The building is well designed and the shells aren't very powerful. As long as we stay on this side of the hotel we're OK."

A voice from the balcony above us boomed. "Hey, Josie, Dos, enjoying the fireworks?" It was Hemingway leaning over the railing. He was grinning broadly, enjoying the show. Tom murmured into my ear, "Josie is Josephine Herbst, the writer you'll be riding with today."

Surprised, I turned to her. "You're Josephine Herbst! I'm Meg Austin. I'll be going to the fiesta with you today with La Pasionaria."

"Oh, how do you do." she said. She gave a wry smile. "We meet in inauspicious times."

Later that morning, Josephine Herbst, still pale and visibly shaken by the shelling that had continued for over thirty minutes, met me in the plaster and glass-strewn atrium of the Florida. Herbst heard me speaking Spanish to a man who was sweeping up the debris. "Your Spanish has a Mexican accent."

I explained how I had learned the language from our Mexican housekeeper. Herbst then told me that she picked up some Spanish when she lived in Mexico for a few months and later on a journalistic stint in Cuba, but that she wasn't fluent in the language and she was hoping I would translate for her. I remembered reading her articles about Cuba in *The New Masses*, an openly Communist magazine about two years earlier. I had been impressed by Herbst's bravery. She was the only journalist to go to the rebel camp in the Cuban Sierra. Her descriptions had been vivid and moving.

Now a soldier in the uniform of the 5th Regiment strode into the hotel and introduced himself as Sgt José and asked if we were comaradas Josefina y Margarita. We rose, murmured our greetings and followed him to the black Citroen that had pulled up to the curb in front of the hotel. The soldier opened the back door for us. Dolores, who was sitting in front, turned and said, "Comarada Josefina, amaneció bién?"

I grinned. Dolores had asked if the dawn broke well, was she awakened well, the usual morning greeting. Josie obviously spoke enough Spanish to understand Pasionaria's question. "Si," she said with a wry laugh, making quick eye contact with me.

Dolores gave us a puzzled stare. I described the shelling of the hotel at daybreak to Dolores, adding that it was during the excitement of that event we had met.

Dolores gave a lusty laugh. "Welcome to Madrid! I'm sorry your first awakening was so shocking, Josefina." She shrugged. "At least you both met. I thought it would be good for the two of you to become acquainted. Josefina will be broadcasting from Telefonica to America, just as you do, Margarita. I thought you might be able to help her get started."

I was surprised to hear this and turned to Josie. "You'll be broadcasting to the States? For one of the networks?"

"Broadcasting, yes, but not for the networks. For Radio Madrid. They hope I can persuade Americans to help the Republic's cause."

Pasionaria was nodding. "Radio Madrid, sí, para los americanos." She then added that they had met in Valencia. "Foreign Minister Alvarez del Vayo introduced us and asked me to give the comrade any assistance she needed," Pasionaria then excused herself, and extracting documents from her satchel, said she needed to peruse some paperwork while they were driving to the fiesta. "Yo soy deputada, y tengo mis tareas."

While Dolores studied her papers, I was able to talk to Josie. I was curious about Herbst's connection to the Communist Party. When I told Tom and Ralph Fitzgerald and some of the other American reporters that I would be riding to the fiesta with Herbst, they told me some of the gossip about her. Apparently, she was recently divorced from a very active Communist writer, John Hermann. They both had taken part in farmers' strikes and championed the Farmer's Committee for Action. In August of last year Tom had met John Hermann at a Party fund raiser for Earl Browder, who was running for President on the Communist ticket. Tom had witnessed Hermann in a huddled conversation with men who Tom was told were members of the Communist underground. Tom said he hadn't understood why they needed to go underground, since the Communist Party was legal, that it caused him to wonder if Hermann were a Russian agent.

Herbst didn't admit to being a member of the Party, Tom said, but was most certainly a radical. Had she been recruited to come to Spain by Comintern, I wondered? It was one of those questions I couldn't ask. I would proceed slowly. "So you just came from Valencia?" I asked, finally.

"Yes, I traveled from Paris directly to Valencia. I needed to contact Alvarez del Vayo. He gave me my instructions and a sheaf of safe conduct passes. When I was driven to Madrid I learned why. We were stopped at countless roadblocks, and men in a confusing variety of militias scrutinized each document as if I might be Franco, himself." Her face had taken on some color as she spoke, but she was still tense. She gripped her purse tightly on her tweed-covered lap, and her cornflower blue eyes darted nervously from side to side as we passed through ruined streets into the countryside. It was a beautiful day—sunny, with a vivid blue sky. Children played in the rubble, climbing over bricks, sifting plaster dust as if it were sand. Sunshine gave the ruins an almost benign appearance.

Beyond the city, the fields were bare, but green. Weeds were sprouting around the sandbags on the ditches that had been used as trenches during the assault on Madrid four months earlier. A few wildflowers had blossomed in the April sunlight. Josie turned to me, her sharp eyes questioning. "There was fighting here?"

"Yes. Thousands of men died here."

Somberly, she surveyed the fields surrounding us, but didn't speak.

I cranked open the car window to smell the air, which was redolent with the fragrance of damp earth and new grass. No gritty cement dust or scent of gunpowder blew into the car. I breathed deeply. Herbst turned away from the battlefield and fixed her eyes on me. "Miss Austin, you seem very young to be a war correspondent."

I laughed. "You mean what's a nice American girl like me doing in a place like this?"

"Not exactly, Miss Austin, but most reporters have more experience under their belts before they get this kind of assignment." I told her I worked in New York as a production assistant for the broadcast journalist, Tom Wells at NBC. "I speak Spanish and Tom persuaded the bosses to let me come with him."

Herbst tilted her head to one side and gave me a knowing look. "You don't sound like a New Yorker, Miss Austin. Where in the States are you from?"

"California. Across the bay from San Francisco. I went to Cal Berkeley, but please call me Meg."

She then broke into a smile. "I, too, graduated from U.C. Berkeley—in 1918. For my senior year, but I'm originally from Sioux City, Iowa."

We had come to a roadblock. A leather-faced old soldier of the Popular Army demanded our travel passes. When La Pasionaria glanced up at him from the document she was studying, the soldier took a sharp intake of breath, made the sign of the cross, and then remembering his training, saluted smartly. "La Pasionaria" he cried. "Pasen adelante comaradas!" She bestowed a beaming smile on him as we drove away.

We passed through the gate of an ancient wall to the royal hunting grounds and heard band music in the distance. The property had been taken over as a training ground for the XVth International Brigade, which would now be part of the Popular Army. A parade would take place on a field near the Duke's castle before the celebratory banquet.

The music grew louder as we bumped along the rutted dirt road. Leaving the car, we joined the crowd of spectators watching the parade.

The snow-topped mountains of the Guadarrama served as a backdrop to the scene. The Spanish and Russian officers were standing on a platform draped with bunting. General Miaja and General Goriev stood side by side returning the salutes of the soldiers as they passed the reviewing stand.

As I watched the Americans and Canadians march by I felt proud to be their compatriot. Many of these men were my age or younger. Most had a worn look about them. Their khaki uniforms were no longer new and their marching was not precise. Their lines were crooked and one or two men were out of step, but it seemed to me they looked brave and determined. They had recently won the battle of Guadalajara, their first clear victory in months, and they were fighting for something they truly believed in. There was a scattering of black faces among them. I had talked to several wounded American Brigaders at the hospital. Most had been unemployed workers, victims of the Depression, who had told me they believed the Communist Party would bring about change and justice for the workingman.

As I watched I couldn't keep from thinking about the boys who were not here, the ones who died fighting, those who died because they didn't have enough weapons, tanks or air cover. If only our government could be convinced to lift the ban on sending weapons to Spain. Would my broadcasts and written pieces be effective? Was there anything I could do to bring about change? If Americans could be here at this moment and witness the resolve of these brave young men, they would open their hearts—or would they?

Herbst was standing next to me, quietly observing the scene. Pasionaria had moved toward Koltsov and another man I had not met, who wore a smartly tailored suit with a French cut to it. He and Herbst had greeted each other briefly when we joined the parade watchers. He spoke English with a German accent.

The band was now playing the catchy tune *The Four Insurgent Generals*. Hemingway had arrived, a Spanish black beret perched jauntily on his head. He gave Herbst a bear hug and a loud kiss. She turned to him, and glancing quickly at me, said, "Meg, I need to talk to Hem a minute. If Dolores wants me will you call me?"

I agreed and watched as the two walked several feet away toward the parked cars. The music was loud and I wasn't able to hear what they were saying. Herbst was peering up into Hemingway's face, her expression tense, her hands fluttering as she spoke. Hemingway had stopped smiling.

The parade was over and the guests began to move up the graveled path to the castle. Dos Passos was among them. Koltsov and the man in the French suit with the German accent were engrossed in conversation as they proceeded up the path. Tom had caught sight of me in the crowd and hurried toward me. "Did you see that man talking to Koltsov?" he asked, touching my arm.

"Yes. Who is he? Josie spoke to him but didn't introduce me."

"It's Otto Katz. He writes propaganda for Comintern and was involved in the recruitment of volunteers for the Brigades. He runs Agence Espagne, a press office in Paris, a front for Comintern. I met him when we were in Paris on our way to Spain. He's German. Persona non grata, of course."

How did Tom know so much about these people, I wondered?

"But where's Herbst? Has she abandoned you?"

"No. She's over there by the blue Renault. Talking to Hemingway." We both eyed the pair. Hemingway was frowning. Herbst was still regaling him with a stream of words. Suddenly, she turned away from him and walked back to my side. I introduced her to Tom, but she barely acknowledged him. Her skin had become pale, her eyes troubled. Tom excused himself and moved up the path with his group of reporters. I noted Hemingway and Koltsov trailing behind, deep in conversation.

Pasionaria swooped toward Hebst and me. "Come. We must go."

When we reached the castle, we walked through a patio decorated with flowering pink oleanders in terracotta pots. We followed the crowd through the huge kitchen smelling of roasting meats, onions and garlic. Pots bubbled on the stove, watched over by a battalion of sunburned young soldiers. My stomach rumbled. I hadn't seen so much food in months. From the kitchen we entered the elegant banqueting hall. Dark ancestral portraits of Spanish grandees with ruffs and swords looked down upon us.

Two military officers decked out with medals welcomed the guests. Soldiers guided us to our places at the refectory tables. At the head table were Generals Miaja and Goriev, five other high ranking officers and La Pasionaria. Herbst and I were seated at the table next to it. Hemingway and Dos Passos were across from us but closer to the generals. I looked around for Tom and saw him on the other side of the room with the rest of the press corps. The German in the French suit was next to him. The cast had assembled.

A carafe of red wine was set before me and I poured glasses for both Josie and me. We clinked glasses, "to the 15th Brigade" she said. We were then served steaming plates of paella, fragrant with saffron. Josie slowly picked up her fork, but kept her eyes focused across the table at Hemingway and Dos Passos. I wolfed down the paella, but was distracted by Hemingway's raised voice, which boomed out harsh and mocking. "Dos, you've got to stop this whining about your old buddy Robles. He's dead. Executed. He was a fascist spy."

The word *spy* hung in the air. Josie set down her fork and I stopped eating. Had I heard correctly? I watched Dos Passos stare at Hemingway. "Hem, José Robles could not be a fascist spy. You don't know him! He's loyal to the Republic. He detests Franco. A spy? Impossible."

Hemingway's voice rang out. "You're 100% wrong. Josie and I just heard the truth. He was imprisoned and executed weeks ago." He gulped down half a glass of wine then thrust his fork into his paella.

"Who told you this nonsense?" Dos Passos' voice was low and controlled, with an underlying hint of steel.

Hemingway swallowed his paella. He shrugged. "We can't tell you his name. He's a German correspondent. And we just talked to him. Here at the fiesta."

"Here?" Dos Passos' eyes swept the room.

"Yes, he said we should tell you to stop asking about Robles. Your friend was a traitor. Your continued questioning of everyone in sight is bad for our film. Your zeal for the cause will be questioned."

Dos Passos shook his head. "He's mistaken. Robles is not a traitor!"

"No." Hemingway's tone was self righteous, bullying. "It's you who are mistaken. Stop the hand wringing, the whining, Dos. Robles was shot as a proven fascist collaborator, a dirty spy. He betrayed his friends."

"I want to speak to this German correspondent. Where is he?" Dos Passos' voice remained low and hard.

"He won't talk to you. He doesn't want to have anything to do with you. You were the traitor's friend. Josie and I decided to tell you what he said for your own good."

Mercifully for Dos Passos, Hemingway's tirade was interrupted by General Mejia's toasting the International Brigades, specifically the Fifteenth. Everyone rose and drank. When the toasts had finished, Dos Passos left his place at the table and approached Josie. He leaned down and spoke into her ear, asking her if she had heard what Hem had told him. She nodded, yes she had heard that Robles had been executed.

"As a fascist spy?"

"Yes."

"It's a lie. José Robles is not a fascist!"

Josie took hold of his hand. "Dos. Go to Valencia. Talk to Alvarez del Vayo."

"Josie, I already talked to him. He told me nothing. He said he didn't know what had happened to Robles."

"Well. Talk to him again." Her voice was firm, commanding. What did Josephine Herbst know, I wondered? I remembered that Dolores had said she met Herbst in Valencia, that Alvarez del Vayo had introduced them. Something was odd about this story. I had been with Herbst since we got here. Where was this German correspondent? Was it Otto Katz? But he had not spoken more than two words to Herbst.

I thought of the other assassinations and disappearances I'd heard about from Lance. Had Robles been murdered by the Stalinist secret police? I turned and stared at Josephine Herbst. Then I fixed my eyes on Ernest Hemingway. I watched as he tipped a silver whiskey flask into his mouth. How could such a superb artist be so cruel?

That evening the English-speaking press corps' major topic of conversation concerned the confrontation between the two famous writers. Hemingway's booming voice had been heard throughout the dining room. We had been shocked by his thoughtless bullying. Although there was a difference of opinion amongst the corps about what had happened to Robles, almost all agreed it was inexcusable of Hemingway to have told his good friend, Dos Passos, such terrible news in such a public and unfeeling manner.

Most of us didn't bother with dinner at the Gran Via. We'd stuffed ourselves at the luncheon banquet and couldn't face the restaurant's meager, unappetizing fare. Instead we gathered at Chicote's. Hemingway, Dos Passos and Herbst were not with us and we were free to continue the postmortem about the events of the afternoon. I was asked about Herbst but had little to offer. In the car returning from the fiesta she had avoided talking about what had happened at the banquet between Hemingway and Dos Passos. Or of José Robles. She had changed the subject or feigned sleep whenever I mentioned their names. On our return to Madrid she complained of a headache and disappeared into her room.

Tom and I left Chicote's and strolled back to the Florida. The mild April evening air had only a slight odor of gunpowder and plaster dust. Since the morning's shelling, the artillery had been quiet. It had been an exhausting day, and I couldn't stop thinking about Hemingway's cruelty. I also continued to feel puzzled by his story. Had it been Otto Katz who had told Herbst about Robles' execution as a fascist spy? "Tom, you were sitting with the correspondent you said was Otto Katz. Did he say anything about Robles? Or give any indication that he was the German correspondent who spilled the news to Josie?"

"No. But I believe he knew about it."

I stopped and faced Tom. "What makes you think so? How would he know? Because he works for Comintern?"

Tom drew me into the shadows and peered around us before he spoke. "He writes propaganda for Comintern, yes. I think he knew about Robles. He didn't seem at all surprised by Hemingway's comments to Dos Passos. Katz told me he thought Dos Passos was obsessed, that he should have dropped his persistent inquiries about Robles, that whatever the reasons for Robles' arrest and execution, they would have been necessary."

"You mean—like the executions in Russia? The Terror?"

"If you want to call it that." Tom turned away from me, glancing behind us again, and spoke in a low voice. "Look, Meg, this is not the place to be discussing this." He took hold of my arm and attempted to guide me toward our hotel.

I pulled my arm from his grasp. "Tom, why can't we talk? Are you afraid someone is listening? Are you becoming paranoid like Orlov and Koltsov?"

"Meg, you don't understand. As I've said before, these are terrible times. I just don't want anyone to misconstrue what you're saying."

"You mean someone might accuse me of being a fascist spy?" My voice had become sharp.

"Not exactly, but they might believe you're not to be trusted with certain information."

I stared at Tom, incredulous. "Tom, you're becoming one of them! You don't care if innocent people are accused of being spies and traitors and secretly executed."

He met my look. "I believe in fighting fascism with whatever means is necessary."

Tom's eyes were as hard and cold as a block of granite. He seemed a stranger. I turned from him and fled to the hotel. I felt hurt, angry, confused. I wanted to scream at him, tell him he was making a terrible mistake that he should not be taken in by the Stalinists. I ran up the stairs to my room and locked the door. When Tom knocked I didn't answer. I flopped on my bed and cried. I didn't know how to handle my confused feelings. Were Tom and I going to break up over politics? I rose from the bed and wiped my eyes. I was exhausted. I needed to sleep but spent the night wide-awake. I kept seeing Tom's cold glance and hearing the ominous tone in his voice.

At first light I gave up trying to sleep. I dressed quickly and descended to the atrium for breakfast. The artillery shelling hadn't started yet, and the atrium was almost empty. As I sat at one of the tables, feeling lonely, drinking my watery coffee, I saw Dos Passos crossing the floor carrying two suitcases and dressed for travel. He nodded to me as he walked by. "Are you leaving?" I asked.

"Yes. To Barcelona, Paris then home."

"Qué le vaya bien!"

"Gracias. And keep safe." He shot me a wan smile, nodded and walked to the reception desk. I watched him as he paid his bill, signed the register and went out the door. I felt a wave of depression as the door closed behind him, a sense of defeat. Did I want to go home? Had I had enough of the complications of this civil war, the confusion, the ambiguities?

I sipped my coffee, glancing at the elevator and the stairway expecting to see Tom, wondering what we would say to each other.

Instead, Josephine Herbst emerged from the elevator. She went to the bar for coffee and then, catching sight of me, approached my table. "May I join you?" she asked quietly.

"Of course, Josie. Did you sleep well?"

"Much to my surprise, I did. And no shelling this morning."

"No, thank God. After yesterday we need a break." I wondered if she knew that Dos Passos had left for the States just a few minutes before, but refrained from mentioning it.

"Meg, I need to do my broadcast later this morning." She pulled a notebook from her bag. "Will you help me deal with Barea, the censor? And then show me where to go at Telefonica?"

I agreed, relieved to have work to do, but continuing to keep my eye out for Tom. Finally, I saw him walking down the stairs. He stopped when he reached the atrium, looked about, caught my glance and approached. "Meg, Miss Herbst, good morning. Did you sleep well?" He touched my shoulder lightly then shoved his hands in his pockets. We avoided eye contact, but I found myself assenting when he asked if he could join us. Josie's presence would act as a buffer between us. We could postpone any discussion of last night's quarrel.

When we'd finished our coffee, Tom excused himself, saying he had to complete a story he was working on. I assumed he was going to his own room. Herbst hadn't brought her typewriter and I suggested she use mine to write up her piece. "You need two copies," I said, and proceeded to explain the censorship system to her. I spent much of the day guiding her through the procedure. Fortunately, the artillery crew must have taken a day off. Josie was able to broadcast without fearing she would be blown to pieces.

I didn't see Tom again that day until he knocked on my door in the early evening, our usual time to go to dinner. "Come in," I said, feeling tension mount in my throat. I hadn't come to any conclusions about how I would behave toward Tom. I felt my face stiffen as I assumed a mask of unconcern, but could I keep it in place?

Tom entered, hat in hand. "Shall we go to dinner?" His voice was calm but cool. He glanced at my worktable. "So how did it go with Herbst? Did you put her through her paces?"

I nodded and reached for my jacket. Perhaps if we maintained a surface of normalcy we could forget about our differences—or just accept them.

That evening we drank quantities of red wine and listened to the other reporters' reports of the day's news. At first they gossiped about Dos Passos' abrupt departure, speculating about his friendship with Hemingway and the status of the film they were both working on. Then they discussed the war news, most of it bad. Franco's troops were having successes in the Basque region and in Aragon.

Walking back to the hotel, I took hold of Tom's arm. He turned to me, withdrew his arm and held me firmly around the waist. "I missed you today, Meg. I felt like half of me had disappeared."

I fixed my eyes on his. "I know what you mean." I gave him a tentative smile. "Shall we call a truce? After all, we're supposed to maintain impartiality, remember? Maybe we both can try harder." I felt my mask slowly drop away and my breathing relax.

Tom laughed softly. "OK. A truce it is. Most certainly a cease fire!" In the blue light from the street lamps, we walked arm in arm back to the hotel, up the elevator and into my room. We managed to keep to our truce for several days, but in 1937 Spain it was not easy to do. Our relationship had changed. It was no longer as open as it had been, and whenever I heard the rumors about Communist secret prisons or POUM members disappearances, I refrained from talking to Tom about them.

Franco provided us with other subjects to discuss, however—to our dismay. On April 26, only four days after the fiesta, Franco ordered the carpet-bombing of unarmed Guernica in the Basque region. Thousands of civilians were killed. Fellow reporters who witnessed the bombing and managed to return to Madrid a few days later, described the horrible scene. Anthony had been there. "The planes zoomed over the open fields where civilians were trying to escape the bombs," he said. "The German pilots dropped incendiary bombs on them as they ran. On men, women and children—and the cows in the field. Setting fire to them. I was hiding in a ditch nearby and I could hear them screaming. Along with the cows bawling."

It was a horrifying story to broadcast. Both Tom and Josie reported it and I did a written piece about the bombing. Colliers had published two of my stories and I hoped they'd publish this one. Americans needed to know about Franco's bombing of helpless civilians. And if Americans supported the Neutrality Act and were opposed to sending weapons to the Republicans, they should be consistent and stop supplies being sent to Franco's Nationalists. Texaco and Standard Oil were shipping gasoline to Franco for his planes and tanks. General Motors. Studebaker and Ford shipped trucks, and Dupont sent bombs via Germany. I had first heard this report from Pasionaria and hadn't been sure it wasn't false propaganda, but when I heard the same information from the British conservative, Duchess Atholl, I believed it to be true. And I was furious at my government's hypocrisy.

A few days after the bombing of Guernica I received two important letters. I had just come into the hotel from Telefonica when the concierge handed the envelopes to me as I passed the desk. One was from my father. I opened it immediately and began to read. I let out a small cry. He was telling me that he hadn't been well and quite possibly would need a gall bladder operation. He insisted I needn't worry, that his doctor had assured him it wasn't a complicated or particularly dangerous surgery. As I read his typewritten words, I felt a wave of fear. Of course I would worry. I immediately thought about going home to be with him.

I walked toward the bar looking for Tom. I needed to talk to him. The second letter remained unopened in my hand. Tom wasn't difficult to find. His head of thick blond hair stood out among the bald or dark heads of the men standing at the bar. I tapped him on the shoulder and he greeted me with a wide smile. We sat at a table and I gave him my father's letter to read. "I'm thinking I ought to go home."

He read the letter quickly and reached for my hand. "He'll be fine, Meg. My uncle had that operation. He told me there was nothing to it."

I was still holding the unopened letter in my hand. Absentmindedly, I slit the envelope and glanced at its contents. My heart jumped. "My God, Tom. The Fund for Republican Spain wants me to do a series of lectures at universities in the States. Listen to this. *The committee has read your articles and heard your reports on NBC radio. We think that your lectures would draw audiences who would want to hear about your experiences in Madrid.* Then they say they'll pay me for the lectures and my travel expenses." Stunned, I let the letter drop onto the table and gazed at Tom. "I'll have to go home!"

11
Valencia and Barcelona
April, 1937

When I climbed into the blue Citroen that would take me away from Madrid I couldn't keep back my tears. Josie, who had preceded me into the car, thrust her handkerchief into my hand, and Tom, who leaned into the open car window, touched my wet cheek. "You'll be back, Meg. You promised. And be sure to call me from Valencia."

The driver, who introduced himself as Eduardo, started the car, and all I could do was nod. I clamped the handkerchief over my streaming nose as we pulled away from the curb, keeping my eyes focused on Tom who had raised his left arm in a Republican salute, his clenched fist held high. We turned the corner and headed for the highway to Valencia. I blew my nose, mopped my face, and peered out the window at the bomb-scarred buildings on the Gran Via. Josie patted my knee. "You'll come back, I'm sure. You won't be able to stay away."

I wondered. At the moment I felt as if my heart had cracked into pieces like the ruined buildings outside the window. I was leaving Madrid, the courageous men and women I'd met here, the passions of a war I felt worth fighting—and Tom. I was a different person than the girl who had arrived here six months ago in her high-heeled red shoes. I smiled ruefully when I thought of those red shoes. Such innocence. I'd had such romantic notions about being a war correspondent in Spain, but reality struck along with the sounds of the first bomb blast. There is nothing romantic about shivering with fear during an air-raid.

I watched an old man crossing the street and thought of my father.

After I had read his letter the week before, I immediately put in a call to him. He hadn't been sure when he would have surgery, but thought it would be mid-June. It was now the fourth of May. I knew it would take me a few weeks to get home, and when Josie said she would be going to Valencia, that Pasionaria had offered her the use of a car and driver, and that I was welcome to go with her, I immediately accepted. From Valencia I could catch a ride to Barcelona, then the train to the border and on to Paris where I would book passage to New York by ship. I wired the Relief for Spain committee to tell them I'd be available in mid-July and telephoned our NBC bureau chief, explaining the situation and requesting a six-month unpaid leave. At first he was angry. 'What the hell do you think you're doing, Meg?" he spluttered. "Your broadcasts have been well received, and we need you there!"

It took a bit of doing to mollify him, but eventually he agreed to my request. And then there was the question of Tom. He was not happy about my leaving, but under the circumstances couldn't object. We didn't make any promises to each other and for the moment buried our political disagreements. I knew it was a break, but was it a break-up? I didn't know.

Now I peered at a grove of olive trees, their gray-green leaves shimmering in the sunlight. It was good to be out of the wounded city. I scanned the sky for planes. Eduardo, the driver, had been on this road the week before, he'd said. I could see his face in the rear-view mirror. He wore the uniform of the fifth Regiment, but he couldn't be more than nineteen. "Eduardo," I said, "was it in daylight you saw the German air-raid on this road?"

"Sí, comarada. Two weeks ago. It was mid-morning, about 10 o'clock. I heard them coming from the west." Lifting one hand off the steering wheel he pointed to the left. "And I got the hell off the road pronto. Drove into an orange grove. I jumped from the car and dove into a ditch at the side of the road just as the planes swooped over, flying low." His eyes connected with mine in the mirror. "Three-engine Junkers. I could see the swastikas on their wings and fuselages. There were peasants in the chickpea field across from the orange grove." He paused, and then in a hoarse voice said, "those chingado low-flying pilots machine-gunned them as they ran. Six people died. Those of us who weren't hit helped the wounded to the nearest farmhouse."

Both Josie and I peered out at the bare chickpea field on our right. Eduardo's tale filled me with a confusing barrage of emotions: anger, despair, fear. I had experienced bombings and witnessed death in Madrid, but the strafing of unarmed civilians was too outrageous to contemplate. Were the pilots who pressed the triggers of the guns fellow-Spaniards? Or were they Germans, Luftwaffe pilots like the ones who machine-gunned the people in Guernica? I closed my eyes, took a deep breath, and tried to dislodge the images of planes, machine-guns, and bleeding victims from my mind. As I had done the day of the fiesta, I opened the car window to allow the clean country air to fill my lungs. "Josie, do you mind the open window?"

She smiled her quiet, rather tight smile. "No indeed. The air's so fresh and warm." She looked up at the sky. "This starched blue Spanish sky. There's nothing like it anywhere. It's hard to believe that German planes could appear at any moment."

I heard that phrase *starched blue sky* and filed it away. Josie had a way with the English language. I glanced at her as she gazed out the window, thinking she was unlike anyone I had known. She kept her own counsel, seeming somewhat sad, as if she had experienced tragedy in her life. Perhaps she was unhappy about her divorce. If so, she never discussed personal matters. She certainly never mentioned Dos Passos or Robles. She was going to Valencia as a journalist following the news.

We had heard there was considerable dissension in the Valencia Parliament. Communist Party deputies were complaining about the Socialist Prime Minister, Largo Caballero. The Communists wanted more power, more control of how the war was being conducted. Many reporters were on there way to Valencia to cover what they expected would be a confrontation between the Socialist and Communist Party members.

We had also heard a report of an uprising in Barcelona. At the daily press briefing the Information Officer had told us that the Anarchists and POUMists were demanding more autonomy in Catalonia. The previous day, fighting had broken out between the Anarchists and government assault troops at Barcelona's Telefonica. The news was troubling. This was no time for the Republicans to fight amongst themselves.

Pasionaria had departed for Valencia the previous day. Before she left she confided to me she'd heard that the uprising in Barcelona was provoked by Nationalist covert agents, Fifth Columnists. "Franco's involved. You can be certain. And the POUMistas are in league with Franco. They're traitors. This counter-revolution must be stopped, the Trotskyists punished." As I listened to her I questioned the accuracy of her report. The terms *Fifth Columnists* and *Trotskyists* immediately caused my spine to stiffen with resistance and disbelief. They evoked thoughts of the existence of firing squads and secret prisons.

Now our driver had slowed as we entered the village Josie wanted to visit. A battalion of the International Brigade was camped nearby. The sky was darkening and we planned to spend the night. We stopped in front of a low stone, black-shuttered building, which the driver told us was a former schoolhouse that now served as a hostel. The shutters needed paint and much of the mortar between the stones had loosened, but red geraniums flourished in terracotta pots on the window ledges.

When we entered, it seemed as every pair of eyes in the room turned to stare at us. Soldiers sat at a long table before plates of eggs and steaming cups of coffee. Village girls served red wine from gleaming pitchers. The table was spread with a white cloth and green netting covered the chandelier above it. The room was dark. No chink of light would be seen from the shuttered windows that would alert the Condor Legion to their presence. One of the soldiers stood by the closed window guarding the pile of backpacks and rifles leaning against the wall.

The men were speaking a jumble of languages. German seemed to be the most prevalent, but I heard languages I didn't recognize. Slavic, perhaps, or Hungarian. They greeted us with boisterous shouts of pleasure. Josie answered them in German, a language in which she was fluent. Unfortunately, I understood none of it. The dueño of the hostel stepped forward and bowed to us, welcoming us, finding places for us to sit at the table. His wife directed us to the outdoor sink and toilet, apologizing for the lack of light. "The bombings." she said, lowering her voice, as if the pilots of the unseen planes might hear her.

At the table, I scanned the faces of the men. They were a battery crew, they told Josie. They looked confident and joyful. Josie leaned toward me and spoke in low tones—in English. "These men have been summoned from the shadow of the cellar, a dark place. Now they are visible."

Josie's elegant language sounded to me like Marxist rhetoric. I assumed she meant that the soldiers had come from countries like Germany and the Balkans where they had lived in oppression and poverty and now were fighting for freedom.

I smiled, and we drank our wine and spooned up the fresh-tasting country eggs. The soldiers eyed me constantly, flirtatiously. I smiled at them but continued to consume my meal. Josie quietly informed me what languages the men were speaking: Yugoslavian, Czech, Hungarian, Romanian, and German, of course.

After the local girls cleared the plates and folded the tablecloth, the table was pushed against the wall and the benches placed around the room. The soldiers gathered on the benches or stood at the back of the room leaning on the wall. Five little girls in white dresses lined up before the men and began to sing. The room became hushed. The girls sang like angels, their voices pure and sweet.

Then the Yugoslavians came forward, laughing heartily. One man led them, pretending to hold a baton. They sang what I assumed was a folk song, and rounded their o's and a's like professional choir singers. There was an accordion solo of *Sole Mio* and a German recited an endless poem that nobody could understand but the Germans. The Czech soldiers sang *Roslein, Roslein* with the tenderness of someone actually serenading his girlfriend. A Hungarian violinist played a gypsy tune, and finally two comic Romanians, stamping and singing, of all things—*Who's afraid of the big bad wolf*—in English.

The children squealed with pleasure and the rest of us laughed, holding our sides, tears streaming from our eyes. The village girls jumped up and down and the soldiers whooped and yelled. By now the older women had finished in the kitchen and had joined us. When the singing stopped they rounded up the girls and children and herded them out the door. As they left, the girls darted glances at the soldiers, dark eyes sparkling, hands fluttering. The soldiers threw them kisses and called out their good-nights. They then collected their bedrolls and rifles and departed to their camp, which was in a field in back of the hostel.

The hostel-keeper's wife ushered us into a room next to the kitchen, which was just large enough for two cots and a washstand. Josie sat on one of the cots and wrapped a blanket around her narrow shoulders. "What an incredible scene," she said. "I felt such a sense of brotherhood in that room tonight."

"And friendship between the villagers and the soldiers."

She glanced at me. "Yes. And joy."

The next morning when I was waiting for our Eduardo, our driver, to finish his breakfast one of the young children in the household stood next to me at the table as I was writing in my notebook. She stared at my pen so intently that I asked her if she wanted to write or draw something. She nodded shyly. I dug out a sheet of typing paper and a pencil from my briefcase and set them before her on the table. Diligently, she bent over her drawing, and I watched the picture emerge. She first drew an outline around her hand, which she had placed at an angle on the paper. Next to the hand she drew a house. In the sky above she sketched airplanes with swastikas on their wings and falling bombs. She then put what looked like rising flames on the ends of the fingers and from the roof of the house. In a corner of the sky she made a circle for the sun and in front of the house she drew a flowerpot with a flower growing from it. Above the airplanes, she placed a floating figure with outspread wings. At the bottom of the page she printed in large letters, *La casa de mi abuela*. My grandmother's house. She pushed the picture away in a business-like fashion and looked up at me. The light from the open door lit her solemn face. The breath caught in my throat.

I asked her if she would give it the picture to me to take home "But keep the pencil," I said, trying to sound cheerful, and I pulled two more sheets of paper from my bag and handed them to her. "Did the airplanes bomb this village?" I asked. Gravely, she nodded. I thanked her and carefully placed her picture in my briefcase next to the notebook that described last night's merriment. It was time to leave.

As we approached Valencia I could smell the oranges. We had driven through the sweetly perfumed air of the blossoming orange groves, but under the trees that lined the streets of the town fruit lay rotting. The sour smell of fermenting fruit was unpleasant. I could also catch the odor of the sea, the Mediterranean, a musty, oily smell, and when we drove by the docks I could see the signs of bombings. Crumbled warehouses and piles of rubble were scattered along the pot-holed road. Wrecked fishing boats lay on their sides next to shattered piers. Very few ships were anchored in the harbor.

I thought of Lance and his rescue efforts. He had said that he brought his endangered refugees to Valencia to flee aboard foreign merchant ships. The shipping blockade would have stopped that exodus. How did they escape the country now? Over the French border?

Now I looked up at the sky that had become overcast. Dark clouds moved slowly overhead, and a bank of fog crept across the sea toward land, which meant the Condor Legion could not fly. We need not fear air-raids—for the moment, at least. Eduardo drove us first to the undamaged Hotel Metropole. "Wait here a moment Comarada Josefina, and I'll find out where they want you to go."

As I glanced up at the hotel I spied the red Russian flag flying over the front door. I turned to Josie. "The Russian consulate?"

Josie nodded.

I stared out the window at the red flag. I was still wondering about Josie's connections to the Communist Party and the Russians. She had come to Valencia before she arrived in Madrid. Certainly, Pasionaria had been treating her as a very important visitor. It wasn't every journalist who was offered a car and driver to go to Valencia. Then there were the broadcasts that had been arranged for her to do by the government information office. And there were those 1934 articles about Cuban rebels in the *New Masses*. Josie was such a quiet, mouse-like person it would seem impossible to consider she could be an agent for Comintern. But then, why not? I could smell a story here, but couldn't 't touch it. I was leaving Spain.

Now Eduardo climbed back into the car and told us we would be going to the Hotel Victoria where most of the other journalists were staying. "I'm to tell you, Comarada Josefina, that Foreign Minister Alvarez del Vayo will meet you there this evening."

Josie sighed. "I hope the hotel has hot water. I'm dying for a good bath. And a good night's sleep."

"And something to eat," I added. I'd heard that food was difficult to obtain in Valencia because of the blockade. The foreign merchant ships that normally delivered supplies were being sunk by Italian submarines and bombers. Eight British merchant vessels had been sunk by the Italians—and the Brits had barely complained to the Italian government. It was impossible to understand. Did they want Italy as an ally that badly?

As we registered at the desk I heard my name being called. It was

Ralph Fitzgerald. He looked thinner, but his brown eyes were as sharp as ever. He gave me a hug. "I hear you're on the way home. You got here OK. No Junkers?"

"None. Thank God. So, Ralph, how long have you been here. Anything happening?"

"I've been here ten days. And all hell's breaking loose in Parliament. We've been taking bets on how much longer Largo Caballero will be Prime Minister. People are talking about Negrín being next. But the biggest story is happening in Barcelona. It's hard to figure who's fighting who."

"I know. Pasionaria claims it's the fascists. Agents provocateurs. Fifth Columnists helped by POUM."

"Yeah, she would say that. Sounds like her usual propaganda. A couple of the boys and I have found us a car to drive up there. We can make room for you if you'd like to hitch a ride. We're leaving tomorrow."

"Great. I can catch a train in Barcelona. I hope! If they're still running."

"The last I heard there's a train going to the border almost every day."

"Almost?"

"Well, you know how it is. Se depende."

"Ralph, where do I find a phone? I promised to call Tom between 8 and 10 tonight."

"You can call Madrid from here in the hotel. There's a phone next to the reception desk." He tilted his head to one side and gave me a mischievous glance. "So you're still hooked up with that broadcast hack?"

I hesitated, then nodded. "Yeah, I guess."

Josie had finished registering and stepped to my side. I introduced her to Ralph. They exchanged greetings, but Josie didn't remain to chat. "I'm going to my room, Meg." She looked at the number tag on her metal key. It's 107. I'll meet you later."

But I didn't meet her later. I only caught a glimpse of her that evening in front of the hotel as she was being helped into an elegant Hispano Swiza by Alvarez del Vayo. Early the next morning I left

Valencia with Ralph and two other journalists. Josie's connection to the Robles/Dos Passos/ Alvarez del Vayo story was to remain a mystery.

The ride to Barcelona was long but uneventful. Fog clung to the coast, a cloud cover that, lucky for us, kept the Condor Legion grounded. The driver, José, was in his fifties and was a seasoned chauffeur. Ralph and the other two journalists slept much of the trip. I sat squeezed between Ralph and a Canadian called Mountie. Mountie wrote for the *Toronto Sun*. He had red hair and a neatly trimmed red mustache. His eyes were a piercing blue. Jerry Miller, a young reporter for the *New York Times* sat in front.

When I had called Tom on the hotel phone from Valencia he had asked me to call him again from Barcelona any evening after 9 PM at the Florida. At the moment the Anarchists were still in control of the Telephone Exchange in Barcelona, he said, and the calls to Madrid were still going through. He needed me to dig out the latest news. "What the hell is happening there? As soon as I'm sure the Telephone Exchange is functioning, I'll go to Barcelona myself. I can do my broadcasts from there as well as Madrid, but not if the Anarchists are preventing access."

We approached Barcelona on the coastal highway from the south. It was May 5th, two days after the beginning of the armed conflict in the city. To my surprise, through the fog I spied two low gray ships sailing into the harbor. Ralph pulled out his binoculars and peered at the vessels. "British destroyers!" he cried. "What the hell!"

Mountie was reaching for the binoculars. "Let's have a look! You're right. They're flying the Union Jack." He handed me the glasses, and I could see the flag clearly—and the formidable cannons protruding from the decks. I returned the binoculars to Ralph. "Are they here to evacuate their nationals?"

"Who knows?" Mountie said. "Maybe old Chamberlain is scared the Anarchists will take over Europe!" He handed the glasses to Jerry, who was now wide awake.

As we drove into the town, the streets were eerily quiet. This was not the Barcelona I remembered. On the Ramblas, the main street, shops' steel shutters were tightly closed, and the wooden window shutters of the apartments on upper floors were also shut. I felt a prickling of fright run down my spine. A man was scurrying along the sidewalk, hugging the wall, dodging from doorway to doorway, waving a white handkerchief over his head. We drove around an empty tram, its doors closed, abandoned at an intersection. A rattle of rifle fire split the air— and then an answering volley.

José made a quick turn onto a side street. "Maybe it's safer off the Ramblas," he said. Almost immediately we came upon a sandbagged barricade. We were stopped by a young man in blue coveralls, a black and red panuela around his neck, pointing a rifle at us. I noted a hand grenade hanging from his leather belt. "Journalists!" Ralph shouted. "We all held up our credentials. "We're going to the Hotel Continental."

The guard waved us around the barricade and two blocks further we arrived at the side door of the Continental. We had been told before we left Valencia that the Continental had been taken over by the Generalité, the Catalan government, and had been declared neutral ground and was the place we should make our headquarters.

The only beds available were cots placed in small rooms in back of the dining room. I shared a closet-sized space with two chicly dressed Spanish women who eyed me with suspicion when I entered the cubicle. I introduced myself. Peering around the tiny space I smiled. "Not much room, is there."

One of the women responded politely but coolly, agreeing that indeed the room was *very* small. She turned away and continued to adjust her makeup in the mirror of her gold compact. The second woman gave me a brief nod and then left the room. I shrugged, shoved my suitcase and typewriter under the cot and went out into the lobby, looking for Ralph, Jerry or Mountie.

I spied Ralph and Mountie at the bar, joined them there and surveyed the crowd. The front window of the dining room had been hit by gunfire and that section was closed off. From the street outside the hotel I could hear sporadic volleys of gunfire—then silence. I listened for artillery and machine guns, but the shots fired were from rifles. I had become an expert in distinguishing between weapons, a skill I hadn't wanted to learn. I judged that if I stayed in the hotel and away from the windows I would be safe—unless the shootout escalated into a full-scale war. It was not a comforting thought.

The hotel was jammed with an astonishing assortment of people. I recognized some of the foreign journalists clustered at the bar. Sitting next to me an American pilot introduced himself who said he was flying for the Republic. Then Mountie pointed out several Communist agents "That one over there—the one in the white suit—is a spy for OGPU. Reporters call him Charlie Chan." Two wounded soldiers of the International Brigade sat in wicker chairs nearby. One of the Brigaders' head and left eye were swathed in bandages and the other's arm was in a sling. In a corner of the room a gang of noisy, rough-looking men huddled around a table cluttered with pitchers of red wine. "They're truck drivers who were carrying oranges back to France," Mountie said. "They were stopped by the fighting." At another table I saw nattily dressed Spaniards, their cream-colored suits expertly tailored, who looked like they could be fascist sympathizers! How absolutely insane, I thought. Bizarre. And outside on rooftops men were shooting at each other from behind mattresses.

Remembering my job as a reporter, I asked questions of everyone I spoke to. "How did the fighting begin?" I asked. The answers were confusing and contradictory. Several hours later when I sat with Ralph and Mountie waiting for the waiter to bring our food, I had arrived at some sense of what had happened. The three of us compared notes. We pulled out our notebooks. "OK, what are the facts?" Ralph said. He unscrewed the cap on his fountain pen. "Number One." he wrote. First, we know the telephone exchange has been controlled by a committee of Anarchists and Socialists."

"Right. Since the uprising," I said. "A whole year—and it's worked well. And peacefully."

"And, two," Ralph said, It's a fact that of all the political parties in Catalonia, the Anarchists have by far the greatest number of members."

"And," said Mountie, "the Communists and Anarchists are in a power struggle."

"Furthermore," Ralph added, "The members of all these groups are armed." He turned the pages of his notebook. "And on April 27 the Anarchists and the Trotskyists were ordered to surrender their weapons. They refused."

"Who gave the order?"

"The Commissioner of Public Order of the Catalan government, a Communist." Ralph continued, checking his notes. "On May 3, the

Communist police chief, Salas, arrived at the Telephone Exchange with three truckloads of armed guards. They grabbed the Anarchist sentries but were shot at from the upper floors by Anarchist machine gun fire."

"So that's how it began?" I asked.

"Right. News of the incident spread within minutes. Barcelonans snatched up their guns, put up barricades, and fired at the police."

The waiter arrived with a pitcher of red wine and our meager dinner of lentil soup, sardines and oranges, the only food the hotel could serve us. We put away our notebooks. I was very much aware of the sporadic rifle fire on the street outside the hotel. I was trapped in a kind of limbo. How would I leave Barcelona?

Soon after I had compared notes with Ralph and Mountie I telephoned Tom and told him what I'd learned. He reported that he'd heard that Largo Caballero had ordered two destroyers to Barcelona packed with a troop of assault guards. He hoped that full-scale war wouldn't break out. "Meg, stay where you are until the fighting stops. Please! The trains might not be running, and if they are they'll be taken over by soldiers. I'll be in Barcelona in about three days if I can find a car to take me. I hope you'll still be there! I miss you, Meg."

"I'll stay until the fighting stops, Tom, but then I'll have to go. I miss you, too, but..." The line became filled with static and then was cut off. I replaced the earpiece onto its receiver. I did miss Tom. It had seemed strange and lonely here without him. Although I'd been on my own in Madrid when Tom was in the field, I always anticipated his return with pleasure. He had brought excitement into my life, and we'd been through so much together.

As I wended my way through the crowded lobby, I accidentally bumped into a blonde, fair skinned young woman I'd noticed earlier. "Oh, sorry" I said in English.

"It's perfectly all right," she said smiling, speaking in a fluting British accent. She was dressed in a plain gray flannel skirt and a rose cotton blouse that reflected on her translucent skin. We both stood still a moment, waiting for a group of well-dressed Spaniards to pass by.

"You're English," I said. "A reporter?" I realized that English women weren't always willing to chat with strangers, but she was the only other

English-speaking woman I'd seen in the hotel. "I'm a reporter for NBC radio. Meg Austin."

We shook hands and exchanged polite greetings. "Ann Blair," she said. "And to answer your question, I'm not a journalist. I'm a journalist's wife." Then she gave a wry laugh. "Actually, I'm a militiaman's wife. My husband came to Barcelona as a freelance reporter, but decided to fight Franco with guns not words. He's been fighting on the Aragon front with the POUM militia." She paused. "I say, won't you join me for a cup of tea? I haven't had a woman who speaks my language to talk to for ages."

"I'd be happy to," I answered. With difficulty we found a small table in a corner of the crowded dining area and caught the eye of a frantically busy waiter and gave him our order. "You say your husband is fighting on the Aragon front. Huesca?"

"Yes. Actually, at the moment he's here in Barcelona—-supposedly on leave, but when the shooting started he hurried to the POUM headquarters to help guard it from the asaltos. He's at the Hotel Falcon, two doors away, so when he can get away he comes here to eat. I've been waiting for him all afternoon."

We then exchanged information about ourselves. I told her I was leaving Spain, about my father and the lectures I would be giving in the States. We complained about the shortsighted Non-Intervention Pact agreed to by Britain, France and America. And we discussed politics in Spain and Barcelona and Europe. We both had similar doubts about the Stalinists but were ardent in our hatred of Franco and Hitler. She told me her husband was a writer and had published two books under the pseudonym of George Orwell. I was surprised—and impressed. I had read his book *Down and Out in London and Paris*.

Suddenly Mrs. Blair's eyes lit up. She jumped up and rushed to a tall, lanky man in a tattered uniform and hugged him tightly. She linked her arm in his and drew him to the table. She introduced him as Eric Blair, and told him I was a journalist returning to the States to give lectures to groups raising money for Spanish Republican relief. He shook my hand, apologizing for his grimy appearance. He spoke with an accent I had leaned to recognize as Etonian, which surprised me. His book had been about being poor, which didn't quite match his fluting English—nor did his rounded Etonian tones fit his ravaged face and ragged clothes. His cap, which he had removed from his unkempt hair, looked as if it had been trampled by a herd of elephants and I could see his bare toes poking from his ruined boots. He smiled at his wife, but his eyes seemed filled with pain. "I'm starved," he said, dropping into a chair that Mrs. Blair had borrowed from the next table.

"There's not much to eat," Mrs. Blair said. "Lentil soup, wine—-maybe sardines, and no bread. Oranges, of course, from the truck drivers, but I did scrounge some cigarettes, Lucky Strikes." Eagerly he lit a cigarette, savoring it, drawing in the smoke into his lungs as if it would give him sustenance. She held out the pack to me, but I refused, not wanting to deprive them of their precious cigarettes. Mrs. Blair then asked him about what was happening outside. "Are you still being shot at?"

"Sporadically. The asaltos are still on the roof at Cafe Moka, the building opposite ours at the Hotel Falcon. Like us, they're shooting from behind stacks of mattresses on the roof. But I don't think they really want to hit any of us. We're all fighting defensively. The Communists are on the roof of the Hotel Colon behind their pile of mattresses. The explosions of grenades seems to have stopped and there's never been artillery fire. We're all exhausted. This internecine spat is insane. We'd all rather be shooting the fascists."

I told him I'd heard that troops of assault guards were on their way from Valencia. "It appears that the central government will be in control of Catalonia soon," I said. We then discussed the dissension between the various parties, the Stalinist push for centralization, Stalin's violent hatred of Trotsky and the lies about POUM.

"I'm about to try to join the International Brigade," he said. "If they'll have me. It would seem it might not be healthy to stick with POUM. A friend told me he'd just received information the Government was about to outlaw POUM and declare a state of war upon it. Trotskyists are being put up against the wall in Russia, and it seems POUMistas in Spain will be next."

Mrs. Blair covered his hand with hers and then called to the waiter who was rushing by. He brought us all wine and removed the tea things. Blair leaned back in his wicker chair and stretched out his long legs. "So, Miss Austin, when you stand before your American countrymen what will you tell them about Spain?"

What indeed?

The next two days were calmer. Suddenly, the trams were running and people went out into the street to attempt to buy food, although almost nothing was left in the shops. The barricades hadn't yet been taken down, and the rooftops were still manned by snipers. An occasional shot was heard, but no grenades. I began to think seriously of making my way to the train station. First I had to find out if the trains to Port Bou were running.

I telephoned Tom to report that the trams were running and I told him about the varied stories that were circulating. He confirmed the rumor about the troops that were on their way. He had lined up a car and driver and hoped to leave Madrid in two days. "Meg, you'll stay until I arrive, won't you?" he pleaded.

"Tom, I don't know. If the trains are running, and if the shooting has truly stopped, I really need to leave. I do miss you, but my father…" Again, the sound faded and crackled. We shouted our good-byes. I felt an empty feeling in my gut. What if something happened to him while I was gone? He was so fearless. Or what if something prevented me from returning? I didn't appreciate his defense of the Stalinists, but I still loved him—and truly missed him.

That evening the assault troops that Tom had told me about arrived from Valencia. They patrolled the streets in groups of ten—tall men in gray or blue uniforms with long rifles slung over their shoulders and a sub-machine gun to each group. I never discovered exactly how many they were, but they were everywhere. The foreign newspapers also arrived, their stories partisan and wildly inaccurate.

I thought of Eric Blair, who I wanted to call George Orwell, and how he had asked me what I would say to my compatriots about Republican Spain. I wondered what he would do now? And what will he say to his compatriots if and when he returns to England?

In spite of Tom's pleading for me to stay until he arrived, I decided to depart this confusing, upsetting country—for a while, at least. I should catch the train to Port Bou while it was still running. The concierge told me would leave at 7:30 the next morning. I bade farewell to Ralph and Mountie and promised to visit Ann Blair in England when the Civil War was over. A weary Eric Blair/George Orwell had returned to the front no longer a naïve idealist, but still with POUM.

12
Barcelona to Paris
May, 1937

That evening I wrote a short note to Tom apologizing for my departure before his arrival, wishing him luck, and telling him I'd return to Spain in a few months. I left the note with the concierge and took a taxi to the railroad station. Although many of the barricades had been removed, the streets were rough and uneven. My driver joked that it was easier to pry up Barcelona's paving stones than it was to put them back together again.

The train for Port Bou was waiting on track number six. I purchased my second-class ticket to Paris, walked down the number six platform and found my compartment. I noted the dining car three cars in back of mine. I examined my ticket. I knew I would have to change trains at the border, since the gauge on the French tracks was not the same as the Spanish.

My compartment was empty and it seemed strange not to have a willing male to lift my suitcase and typewriter up into the luggage rack above my seat. I shook off that brief moment of loneliness and settled onto my seat by the window. I inspected my precious passport. Thanks to the American Consul in Madrid my documents were in order—I hoped. He had helped me acquire the visas I needed. I examined my French visa. Crossing the Spanish border into France was not always easy, I'd heard. France did not welcome Spanish refugees. However, I was an American, a documented journalist, and ought not to hassled.

All the same, I was nervous. It didn't help that the train did not depart on time.

It hit me with a jolt that I was actually leaving Spain—and Tom. I knew I could have stayed until the next day to see him, but I couldn't face another good-bye scene. It hurt too much and was too confusing. As I sat peering out the window of my empty compartment, I felt alone and vulnerable. At the same time I was excited at the thought of my new independence.

I straightened my spine and watched a troop of tattered soldiers, some who looked no older than fourteen, clamber onto the train on track opposite from mine. It was headed for Barbastro in Aragon, which was near the front line. They hoisted their heavy packs up the steps into the carriage one by one. I thought of Eric Blair, hoping he would survive both the front line fighting and the persecution of POUM. I couldn't erase the image of the pained expression in Blair's eyes.

I pulled my notebook from my leather bag, wanting to write some notes about what I'd seen and heard in Barcelona. As I was unscrewing the cap to my fountain pen, I suddenly realized I must wait until I crossed the border. The Communist censors were serious about what news was transmitted to the outside world. I put the pen away and quickly scanned my notes, scrutinizing them for anything the border guards might consider suspicious and report to the censor. In my suitcase I had packed several photographs I'd taken of the damage done in Madrid by the Condor Legion. Barea, the censor, had stamped them as acceptable to be shown outside Spain, but in my notes there should be no mention of Russian equipment or personnel, I remembered. Certainly, no notes about POUM or atrocities committed by the Republic, or that men like Orlov were Russian secret police. Lance's description of the murdered political prisoners was burned into my brain. And where was Lance now? Had he escaped detection while helping Spaniards flee Spain?

I glanced at my watch. 8:15. We should have departed forty-five minutes ago. The train with the soldiers going to the Aragon front had chugged away almost as soon as the men had climbed aboard. Now baggage was being trundled down the platform by a man in blue coveralls, but only a scattering of passengers walked by, searching for the appropriate car. Another ten minutes passed. Agitated, I hopped up from my seat and stood in the corridor, peering out the windows on other side of the train. Suddenly, three small middle-aged women loaded with large bundles pushed their way down the corridor and entered my compartment. I returned to my seat, to claim it. Then two elderly men limped into the compartment, their wooden canes tapping on the metal floor. We exchanged greetings in Spanish. Sighing loudly, the women piled their bundles on the floor at their feet, grumbling in Catalan. At that point the train began to move slowly out of the glass-roofed palace-like station. I looked at my watch 8:30—one hour later departing than posted. My fellow passengers must have known the train would leave an hour late.

We settled into our seats. The train moved more rapidly, and soon we were on the edge of town, passing brick factory buildings. Within minutes the track ran along the coast. At first none of us spoke. We all shifted in our seats, straightening skirts or jackets. Two of the women were dressed in black skirts and blouses, stockings and rope-soled shoes. The third woman was in a flowered cotton dress and black leather shoes worn at the heels. I scanned their faces. All were thin, somewhat gaunt. Both men wore black berets that fit their heads as if they'd slept in them. Their dark trousers were worn at the knees and rope-soled sandals barely protected their wide, gnarled feet. They murmured to each other in Catalan, which I didn't understand.

One of the women's face was a mass of sun hardened, leathery wrinkles. Her round black eyes focused on the passing landscape seemed filled with despair. Later she told me in Spanish that one of her sons was fighting in Aragon. Now her fourteen-year old boy wanted to join the Popular Army. "He helps on the farm," she said. "I don't want him to go, but I know he must." She lived near a village fifty kilometers north of Barcelona and her first language was Catalan.

For a while the train tracks ran next to a narrow road that was crowded with people—men, women and children carrying bundles, babies, pushing wheelbarrows piled with boxes. Some were leading cows on ropes or herding a few sheep before them. I watched as they trudged slowly, doggedly along the road. A few carts pulled by mules or sway-backed horses plodded in the midst of the throng, the carts piled high with chairs and mattresses and the elderly. Refugees, I thought. Going to Barcelona? I bit my lip. What would happen to these people?

The woman sitting across from me whose son was at the front

was also staring at the scene outside our window. "From Aragon," she murmured. "Poor souls. They're escaping Franco's Moors." Our train picked up speed and we lost sight of the road. Moments later the conductor bustled into the compartment to check our tickets. He punched a hole in mine, but the others gave up the stub of their tickets. I was the only one going to the border. All the passengers lived north of the town and would get off the train long before reaching the frontier. They'd been forced to remain in Barcelona with relatives until the shootout stopped, they told me, speaking Spanish. None of them knew exactly who had started it. The two men were members of the Federation of Anarchists and blamed the Communists. The women said they didn't know what had happened. They'd been frightened. They'd heard that 500 people had been killed. "Those idiots should have been shooting the rich fascists, not our fellow Republicans!" the woman in the flowered dress said. They were hungry and would be happy to get home. The train made several stops on the way to the border. One by one my fellow passengers gathered their belongings and departed.

I made my way to the dining car hoping to find something to eat. Food had been picked up at one of the stops and coffee made of chicory, rolls and orange juice was being served. As I sat drinking my ersatz coffee, two Spanish Civil guards walked through the car. They both eyed me from under their peaked caps but didn't ask to see my papers. Soon after I returned to my compartment the train slowed, the conductor hurried through the car announcing that we were arriving at Port Bou. "All passengers must debark." I managed to lug my suitcase and typewriter off their perch above my seat, and grabbing my raincoat, made my way down the steps of the car to the platform.

A young porter approached with a baggage cart and hoisted my luggage onto it. "La frontera," I said, reaching into my purse for my ticket. Now I had one more hurdle. I wasn't at all sure that I'd finished with the Spanish border officials. It was possible that the Civil Guards on the train were scrutinizing the passengers, but I wasn't sure. I followed the porter down the long platform to the glass doors of the station. Outside the building was a cluster of wooden shelters and beyond was a wooden barricade. I could see the blue, white and red French flag fluttering over one of the buildings on the other side of the barricade. The flag of the Spanish Republic flew high above the railroad station.

Beyond that, on the French side of the fence, I could see several tracks and another train. The one to Paris?

The porter led me to the first shelter and placed my baggage on a table. A Spanish official ambled toward me. He glanced briefly at my suitcase and typewriter, but didn't ask me to open it. I held out my passport and my other documents. He examined my photograph, looked up at me, frowned, and then broke into a broad smile. Stamping my passport, he said, "Bien viaje!" The boy lifted my bags onto the cart and wheeled it to an opening next to the barricade. From the other side another porter reached for my bags. I tipped the boy, thanked him and followed the new porter to yet another small shelter. The French official scrutinized my passport and journalist's papers. He then asked me to open my suitcase, which I did. One of my red shoes of the pair I hadn't had the heart to discard had shifted so that its high heel was poking upward. The guard smiled, pushed the shoe back in its corner, stamped my passport and waved me on. "Bienvenue a France!" he said. I thanked him and the porter helped me find my new compartment. As I mounted the steps I felt a mixture of emotions; relief, of course, at having crossed the border so easily, but sadness and sense of emptiness at leaving Spain. I vowed to return as soon as possible.

Several hours later we arrived at the Gare de Lyon in Paris. I took a taxi from the station to the Hotel Dauphine, the same hotel where Tom and I had stayed on our way to Spain. When I tried to book a room, my college French seemed useless. I didn't understand a word of what was being said to me. Tom had spoken French well and I had depended on him. I was missing him terribly. Independence came with a price. Obviously, I should have chosen a different hotel, one that had no connection to Tom and where the staff spoke English. After several attempts, the concierge understood I was asking for a room reservation and handed me a key.

The first thing I did after freshening up a bit was to go to a tobacco shop for some cigarettes and to find something to eat. I was starved. As I walked down the rue Dauphine on my way to the bistro where Tom and I had dined, feeling very much alone. I was a shocked to see so many well-dressed people strolling down the street. And the shops! The windows displaying pastries and cakes, and hundreds of cheeses! Even the boucherie with its artfully arranged pieces of succulent meat made my mouth water. It was getting dark and suddenly street lights flashed on. Lights shone from every window. I felt dizzy with disbelief. No bombs here. Not yet, anyway.

That first night in Paris I eyed the couples sauntering along the Boulevard St Germaine arm in arm and felt envious and lonely. I missed Tom. It didn't seem right to be alone in Paris. But I was hungry, and after stuffing myself with superbly prepared quenelles, tournedos de bouef, and a selection of cheeses: Pont l'Evéque, chevre, St André, accompanied by a bottle of Nouveau Beaujolais and followed by a tarte au pomme and café, I staggered back to my hotel and collapsed into bed. Instead of Tom I dreamed of food.

The next morning, while savoring the breakfast of coffee, croissants and cherry preserves that was brought to my room, I planned my day. I needed to check in at the Paris NBC news bureau and I had to book my passage to New York. Then I would go shopping for clothes to wear on my speaking tour—and have lunch.

On my way to NBC I stopped at Cook's travel agency. The Normandie would be sailing in four days from Le Havre and a cabin was available if I were willing to share it with another woman. I agreed. I also arranged for the train to Le Havre. At NBC a paycheck was waiting for me. The Spanish Relief Committee had also wired money for my passage in care of the NBC office, so I had no financial worries.

I wanted to telephone Tom—or wire him, but I didn't know where he could be reached. Martin Bowen, the Paris bureau chief, said Tom was supposed to be in Barcelona by the next day. "I'll send a message to your hotel as soon as we hear from him." Martin was from Boston and still spoke with a Boston accent. He was not much taller than I, and his paunch was quite visible. I thought of the dinner I'd eaten the evening before.

"Thanks, Martin. And if Tom checks in could you tell him I'm here in Paris, but I'm booked to leave May 12 on the Normandie."

Martin nodded. He then steered me to a chair by his desk and fished a pack of Galloises from his shirt pocket and held it out to me. "But now you must tell me what has been happening in Barcelona." He lit both our cigarettes and continued. " We're receiving contradictory reports: fascist provocateurs, Communist provocateurs, Anarchists. What the hell is going on there?"

I set my burning cigarette into the ashtray, pulled my notebook from my purse and flipped through the pages. I'd written notes about what I'd seen and heard in Barcelona while traveling on the train from the Spanish border. I told him briefly what I'd learned. Then I described the scene, the wild reports, the suspicions."

"Meg, darling, you're not leaving Paris for two days. Tomorrow I want you to do a broadcast from here. About Barcelona. Do you have your typewriter with you? If not, you can use one of ours." He pointed to a desk at the far end of the room, which was unoccupied. He looked at his watch. It's 10AM. Write it up for me today. OK?"

I stared at him. Did I really believe I could write up a report that quickly? Unlike print reporters I hadn't had to work with a deadline since I wrote for the Daily Californian in college. And what could I say? I knew I couldn't refuse. I took a deep breath, glanced down at my notes, stubbed out my cigarette in the ashtray and said, "OK!"

I sat before the typewriter and marshaled my thoughts. I thought of Eric Blair/Orwell's despair at the Communist Party's persecution of Trotsky's sympathizers. I decided to omit that conflict and play down the violence between the Communists and Anarchists. I would say that the internecine armed conflict was brief and that all parties had agreed to put aside their differences and concentrate on fighting their true enemy—-fascism. I was aware that I was omitting much of the truth, thereby slanting the news and discarding my precious objectivity. But what the hell, who could remain objective with Hitler waiting in the wings?

And that's how I spent my two days in Paris. I also dined well. Martin took me out to lunch after he read my piece and again for dinner after my broadcast. Over our meals he grilled me about my experiences in Madrid as well as Barcelona. Off the record I told him what I knew. I mentioned José Robles, Dos Passos and Josephine Herbst, but did not disclose any of Christopher Lance's stories of murdered prisoners or escaping Spaniards. Martin had already heard about the rift between Hemingway and Dos Passos. The two famous writers had just left Paris, and were the gossip of the literary scene. I described the lunch where Hemingway had been such an ass, and I used that phrase.

I told him about the Communist Party's attacks on the Trotskyist party, POUM. Martin nodded. "I'm not surprised. Stalin's running new show trials in Moscow. Now he's purging the Red army as well as Trotsky's followers and anyone else who questions his methods or is perceived as a threat. Generals are being tried and shot. Artists disappear." Martin sipped his Bordeaux and we both remained silent for a moment, as if holding a brief vigil for the people caught in Stalin's net. "Meg, do you think the Republicans can win?"

"If the Non-Intervention Pact is dumped. If France, Britain and America send guns and ammunition for Republican soldiers to shoot with. They're fighting like tigers. But with shoddy rifles. No ammunition. Germany and Italy have not only sent planes and tanks and guns, but their pilots and soldiers are fighting directly for Franco. You heard what happened in Guernica. I saw the German Junkers in the sky over Madrid. And I cowered as their bombs exploded. Italian subs and planes are sinking British merchant ships and the Brits don't do anything about it. Russia is the only country helping the Republicans with guns, planes and tanks, but the armaments come with strings attached."

Martin's expression had darkened. He sighed and called for the check. "Let me walk you back to your hotel, Meg. You have an early train to catch. Maybe you can persuade our Americans to help Republican Spain. But to tell you the truth, I doubt it. It's obvious England and France won't intervene. I don't know who's more pro-fascist, Chamberlain or Deladier." He took my arm and we walked out onto the busy Paris boulevard with its bright lights and dazzling shop windows.

A week later I arrived in New York. The crossing had been pleasant enough, although I couldn't keep thinking about Tom, wishing he were with me, and the luxury of the Normandie was a shock. The bountiful servings of food and wine seemed indecent. The contrast to the devastation of wartime Spain was jarring. I also experienced shock when I plunged into the active life of New York City. In spite of the lingering Great Depression and the presence of men and women selling apples or pencils, the streets were filled with well stocked shops and shoppers loaded with purchases. Restaurants and automats were packed with diners. Fifth Avenue department stores displayed elegant apparel, and the crowded sidewalks were filled with well-dressed people. I was dazed.

Before I caught the train to California I stopped in at both the NBC newsroom at Rockefeller Center and the Spanish Relief headquarters in the Village. My speaking tour itinerary was ready for me and a cable from Tom had just arrived for me at NBC.

He wrote: *Spain not the same without you, Meg. Come back as soon as you can. Let me know how your Dad is doing and good luck with speaking tour. Situation in Barcelona complicated. Big news is Republican government change. Juan Negrín now Prime Minister. Largo Caballero resigned. Communists objected to how he was running the war and refused to remain in his government. Hope to hear from you soon. Send cables or write to the Barcelona Continental Hotel. I love you, Meg. Tom*

As I read Tom's cable, I wondered what was really happening in Barcelona and Valencia. The censor would read everything Tom wrote. He wouldn't be able to tell me what was happening to the Trotskyists, or if the war was not going well. To find that out I'd have to get in touch with reporters returning from Spain. It was disturbing not to know the truth. I tucked Tom's cable into my purse. I would think about Spain later. Now I needed to concentrate on my next task, the trip to California and my father's surgery. I vowed to give my Dad my undivided attention. I'd spoken to him on the phone from New York. "Don't worry, sweetheart, I'm not in any danger," he'd said. "The operation's routine, they tell me. But I'll l be so happy to see you."

The Streamliner train would take four days to arrive in Oakland. I'd booked a Pullman with a lower berth. Leaving Manhattan, the elevated train tracks passed next to tenement buildings. From my window seat I peered into grimy windows and fire escapes fluttering with tattered laundry. An occasional flowerpot brightened a window ledge with a brave geranium or tulip. Outside the metropolitan region, I noted makeshift camps on the edges of towns next to the railroad tracks. Hobos huddled over campfires staring at cooking pots. Beans, I wondered—or coffee? We passed by clusters of makeshift shelters put together with scraps of corrugated metal and cardboard. Women scrubbed clothes in washtubs and ragged children played in the dirt. I thought of the brightly lit Fifth Avenue shops and the luxurious Normandie and felt a surge of anger. Poverty existed in the United States as well as Spain. I felt depressed that President Roosevelt's job programs hadn't helped these people. At least he was trying to help the unemployed and elderly poor with programs like the Works Project Agency, the Conservation Corps, and the Social Security Act. And bombs weren't falling.

I picked up a New York Times someone had left on the seat next to me and read about the strikes in Detroit. The CIO and United Auto Workers had organized a sit-down strike at General Motors. GM bosses accused UAW leader Walter Reuther and CIO president John L. Lewis of being Communists. I sighed. How would I convince Americans to become involved in Spain and drop the Arms Embargo Act when there was so much strife here at home? The Brits and French weren't the only ones terrified of Communism.

The silver train slowed as it traversed the spectacular Sierra slopes and chugged into tunnels cut through granite. Snow covered the highest peaks. I felt a surge of sheer delight when I first caught sight of the rugged mountains. I was home on my very own tierra. The long railroad journey was almost over. We would stop in Sacramento for half an hour, but the next stop would be Oakland. If nothing had gone wrong Dad would be at the station to meet me.

At the Sacramento station I descended from the train to breath some fresh California spring air and purchase a newspaper. I bought a *Sacramento Bee* at the newsstand and scanned the headlines. I was stunned. Ten people had been killed at a plant in Chicago when police opened fire on a group of men and women at a rally near the gates of Republic Steel. Three days earlier United Auto Worker organizers were beaten by Ford's police at the River Rouge plant.

I climbed back onto the stuffy train and returned to my seat. I read the stories about the strikes with a sense of disbelief. For the past six months I had been so absorbed by the Spanish Civil War I had paid little attention to the violence in my own country. I was troubled for my countrymen, but also realized the continuing Depression would not make it easy to collect donations and support for the people of Republican Spain.

As the Streamliner pulled away from the station and crossed the Sacramento River, I stared at an encampment of makeshift shelters. I assumed they were harboring migrant workers from the dust bowl in Oklahoma and Arkansas. Dad had written about the influx of migrant farm workers to California. Barefoot children played amongst old tires and around campfires built of stones and rusty pieces of metal. Next to a shelter built of cardboard and scraps of tin roofing, a dusty black Model T Ford was parked, a rocking chair tied onto its roof with frayed rope. It was a sobering scene. Wasn't the government doing anything to help these people?

The next few days I gave my father my undivided attention, just as I had vowed. It was wonderful to be home and to feel the sheltering warmth of his welcoming hug. His hair had turned quite gray and he'd lost weight, but his blue eyes peering at me over his glasses were as lively and sharp as ever.

"Meg, angel, how I've missed you!" He held me by the shoulders and gave me a piercing look. "You've grown up."

He hugged me again and tears welled in my eyes. "It seems like a million years I've been away, Dad—and lots has happened." I pulled a handkerchief from my jacket pocket and blew my nose. "I want to tell you about Spain, but first I need to know what the doctors say about tomorrow's operation."

Dad brewed us some coffee and we settled in the gazebo in our garden. The wisteria was in bloom and it's lavender flowers hung in a bower around us in the sunlight. Dad stirred sugar into his cup. He explained what he knew about the doctors' prognosis. "And if the surgery goes well, which they say it will, I'll get back to work as soon as I can. I'm still City Editor." He settled his wire-rimmed glasses onto his nose in an almost defiant gesture.

I gave him a teasing smile. "So how do you handle the Gazette owners, the Owens? They're so ardently right-wing conservative. Do they interfere with your reporters—force them to slant the news?" I guiltily thought of my own slanting of the Barcelona shootout story.

"Sometimes, but mostly they're concerned with the editorial page. They're involved in what stories we cover and where they're placed—on what page, or if it's on the front page whether it's above the fold or not. But as long as our reporters maintain a semblance of objectivity, the Owens don't interfere. They're certainly isolationists—and hate Roosevelt—and hope that Franco wins in Spain."

I set down my coffee cup. "They aren't afraid of Hitler?"

"Apparently not. Europe's far away. They *are* afraid of Communists, though—foreign agitators, intellectuals. They think the Communists are infiltrating the unions and the universities, stirring up trouble among the unemployed poor." As Dad spoke, he suddenly frowned with pain. "The gall bladder. I guess I'll go lie down for a while." He held his hand on his side and limped into the house.

He entered the hospital the next day and the following morning underwent surgery. As the doctor assured me when he emerged from the operating room, the procedure had been routine and successful. After a day or two Dad was no longer in much pain and was clamoring to go home. Much to his disgust he was forced to remain in the hospital a full week. Visiting hours were strict and I could see him from 2 to 4 in the afternoon and from 7 to 8:30 in the evening. Nurses were stern. Rules were rules, they said. I thought of the wounded soldiers I had visited in Madrid moaning with pain, lying on stretchers placed on the floor calling for their mothers, and the desperate nurses rushing from patient to patient with no morphine and not enough trained nurses or orderlies to help them.

I received a letter from Tom a few days after Dad's operation. Tom asked about Dad's surgery and said how much he missed me. He did tell me that Negrín had outlawed Trotskyist POUM. I knew that this would be disastrous for the Trotskyists who had fought so hard for the Republic. Orlov's secret police would arrest them. I recalled Orwell's bitter comments about the Stalinists. How would I address that inter-Communist Party conflict on my lecture tour? The question would be asked, for sure. I could only say I didn't know enough to answer, which would be the truth.

I folded Tom's letter and answered it later that day. As I wrote, I wondered where he was. Had he gone to Aragon to cover the fighting there? I listened to the NBC news broadcasts hoping to hear his voice, but he wasn't on, which meant he was in the field somewhere. I felt lonely without him. At the same time, it felt good to be on my own, to be doing my own work.

When I wasn't visiting Dad I worked on my speech for the lecture tour. I had slides made of photographs I'd taken in Madrid during Franco's assault and the child's drawing of the bombing of her grandmother's house. The Spanish Relief organization agreed to provide me with a projector and a volunteer to run it. My first lecture would be at my alma mater in Berkeley. The Political Science department had set a date for me to give a lecture to the students about what was happening in Spain. After my lecture, a cocktail party would be held at a professor's house north of the campus. It would be there that I would appeal for contributions to Spanish War Relief for the orphans and refugees and to buy ambulances.

In the meantime, the news from Spain was dark. I scoured the newspapers for information, often placed on back pages. The *San Francisco Chronicle* and the *Los Angeles Times* covered the civil war most thoroughly, sometimes on the front page. They reported that Franco's troops had taken the northern provinces, Bilbao and the Basque country. Two thirds of Spain now lay in the Nationalists' hands. I didn't want to believe what I was reading, but knew it was true. Franco might win.

13

The States and Paris

June-December, 1937

For the next six months I toured the States giving lectures, talking to anti-fascist groups about the bravery of the Spanish people fighting for their democratically elected government and their desperate need of aid. Most of my talks were given at universities around the country. In Hollywood I spoke to famous actors, writers and directors where most of the funds for war relief were raised. The movie industry had absorbed many refugees from Germany—Jews, Communists, Socialists, artists— or people who abandoned Germany rather than witness the Nazi destruction of freedoms and persecution of non-Aryans. At a meeting sponsored by the Hollywood Anti-Nazi league, which was rumored to be a Comintern organization, I raised $17,000 from seventeen actors. Other donors at universities in other parts of the country were not so financially generous, but were ardent in their support of the Spanish Republic. Invariably the question was asked about the war's atrocities.

In Chicago a man in a workman's cap stood up. "Can you tell us what you know about the atrocities—committed by the Communists and Anarchists—like the killing of priests and nuns?"

I took a deep breath. I spoke carefully, knowing this was an important issue, particularly to American Catholics. "I saw the burned churches in Barcelona and heard eye-witness reports of the killing of priests and nuns that occurred at the time of the generals' insurgency. I heard it from many sources, but I also was told that committees of Anarchist militias put a stop to the killings within a few weeks of the

142

uprising." I told them Pasionaria's accounts of certain priest's' treatment of the poor. I also described my visit to the group of nuns who were being protected by the Communist 5th Regiment.

I showed my photographs of Madrid's bombed buildings and wounded civilians and soldiers. Finally, I showed the slide of the picture the little girl had drawn in the village on the way to Valencia, the drawing of her grandmother's house, the German airplanes and the floating angel.

The lectures were exhausting. Although intellectuals on both coasts and major universities were fiercely opposed to Franco and fascism, I was shocked by the insularity of the majority of my countrymen and women. Spain was too far away. We had our own problems here at home: unemployment, poverty, strikes, lynchings.

It was a relief to return to New York. My talks there were well accepted—and not just at universities. By November of 1937 considerable numbers of refugees from Hitler's persecution had found their circuitous way to New York. New York's anti-fascist groups were passionately active.

I was asked, of course, the question about the rumored secret prisons and the killings of prisoners. My answer was always brief, just as I had planned. "I don't know enough to answer that question." As I spoke I thought of Orwell's asking the same question in Barcelona. It was troubling, but what could I say? "I do know," I added, "about the Nationalist's murder of thousands of civilians and captured soldiers. I heard descriptions of the killings in Malaga and Badajoz and Guernica by many eyewitnesses." I described the death of the child from artillery shrapnel I had seen on the street in front of my hotel in Madrid.

My major problem in New York was trying to keep peace during the discussion period after my lectures. Stalin's purges had wrought havoc within the left-wing anti-fascist groups and the Communist Party. "Stalin has his reasons," one participant would yell, or "the end justifies the means", or "the traitors were arrested and shot because they were fascist spies." Others would shout out "Stalin is betraying the revolution!" On one occasion the organizers of the meeting had to stop a fistfight that broke out in the audience. A woman brought the room to order by beginning to sing the *Internationale*.

I was constantly reminded of Tom's faith in Stalin's methods. Tom and I wrote to each other often. Due to censorship I had to read between the lines in his letters, of course. It was obvious the war was not going well for the Republic. Tom wrote: *The Nationalists' superiority in air power is killing us. The German Junkers have been replaced by a more powerful, faster plane, the Heinkel 111 and now the Messerschmidt 109's are taking out our bombers and fighters. Do you think there's any hope of the U.S. Arms Embargo being repealed?*

Meg, your speaking tour is almost over. When are you returning to Spain? I saw La Pasionaria yesterday and she asked about you. She says she needs you to do your stories about the suffering of the women and orphans—and the bravery of the wounded soldiers in the International Brigade. And I miss you more than you can imagine. I feel as if you are drifting away from me, but I know that Spain is in your blood now. You won't be able to stay away.

I let the thin blue pages flutter into my lap and considered my options. It was true that Spain was in my blood, but did I want to continue my relationship with Tom? In the past six months I had kept men at arm's length, maintaining my independence. I was no longer the same girl who fell in love with glamorous Tom Wells. As Dos Passos had said, I'd been tried by fire. Reality had raised its ugly head.

It was December and my six-month's leave from NBC was up. It was time for me to check in with my boss. With a certain amount of trepidation I approached Rockefeller Center. The cement walkway was slippery with snow and ice. As the elevator zipped up to the newsroom I thought of the winter in Madrid and the wind blowing from the snow-covered Guadarrama mountains—and drinking Spanish brandy in Chicote's with Tom and the boys. Then when I stepped out of the elevator into the newsroom and smelled the familiar mixture of cigarette smoke and burnt coffee and heard the telephones jangling and the teletype machine clicking and the typewriters clattering, I felt a rush of excitement and anticipation. I wanted to get back to work.

My boss, Ben Heller, a short, stocky man who was striding about the studio with quick, vigorous steps, greeted me warmly. In a rush he gave me my orders: Barcelona. "The government has moved there. I want more stories about the wounded soldiers, particularly Americans, and the suffering civilians. Keep it tough and strong. Nothing sentimental. That's what you're good at." He held out a sheaf of papers to me. "And we're giving you a promotion and a raise. You're a full-fledged reporter now."

I found myself beaming at his words. I would be one of the few women journalists in the field—like Gelhorn and Knowles. I thought my heart would burst with pleasure. Then I wondered if I would still be helping Tom. "What about Tom?" I asked. "Do you still want us to work together?"

"Sure. As a team. He'll cover the fighting. Your beat will be the home front."

It was with mixed feelings that I accepted the reality of my assignment. I was thrilled at the promotion—that I was now a bona fide foreign correspondent, not just an assistant at the bottom of the ladder, but one step up. At the same time, I knew that the German planes were bombing Barcelona, and I remembered only too well my terror during the bombardment of Madrid. The image of the dead child in his mother's arms flashed before me. I felt a shiver of fear. At the same time, it had been thrilling. I'd been tested. Could I take it again? And there was Tom.

And it was Tom who two days later I heard broadcast the report that the Republican army had launched an offensive in Aragon and captured the city of Teruel from the Nationalist troops. When I listened to the pride in his voice announcing the victory I could hardly keep from shouting with joy. I wanted to be there, on Spanish earth. As soon as possible!

Two weeks later I walked down the gangplank of the Champlain, which had anchored in the Le Havre harbor. It was mid-January and a frigid wind blew from the Atlantic. It was a relief when I climbed onto the heated train on my way to Paris. I savored the warmth, knowing I would be numb with cold as soon as I arrived in fuel-starved Republican Spain.

On my first day in Paris I went to the NBC office to check in with Martin Bowen. My boss in New York had wired him that I was on my way to Barcelona and that he was to begin the process of acquiring my journalist's documents and visas. Martin gave me the three-times kiss on the cheeks in the French fashion. "Darling, it's so good to see you. I have a packet of papers for you. He pointed to a bundle tied up with blue string sitting in a wire basket on his desk. "We've rounded most of the documents except the exit visa from the French. You'll need to take your passport to the Quai d'Orsay to be stamped." He explained which were the official documents and then held up a fat envelope. I recognized the handwriting. It was a letter from Tom.

I waited until I returned to my hotel before opening the letter. It was typed on onionskin paper and was several pages long. *"When I got your wire and knew that you were really, truly going to be with me soon, I yelled out the news to everyone I saw. I've missed you more than you can ever know and can hardly wait until you arrive."* He then wrote about how much he loved me, which I read slowly. *"I remember those nights walking arm in arm in the blue light of the Gran Via, mellow from drinking Spanish brandy at Chicote's, knowing we would soon climb the stairs to your room. As I write these words I can smell your skin, hear your voice. Jesus, Meg, how I love you."* I knew I needed time to ponder his words and consider my response. I remembered the romance, but I also recalled the reality—how often we quarreled as we walked and how the boom of artillery fire drowned out the sound of music.

The remainder of his letter was about his presence at the battle of Teruel. *It was surreal. The red-brown mountains surrounding us were patched with white. Ralph Fitzgerald and I crouched in a ditch, shivering with cold. I could see the Brigaders crawling like crabs over icy rocks. Bombers dived and the men were mowed down by machine gun fire. Others crawled on. Then the blizzard hit. The wind blew snow into my mouth and eyes and it kept getting stronger. I've never been so cold in my life—chilled to the bone. Within minutes the bodies of the fallen men were buried in the snow. But no planes were flying. The men continued to advance. We kept to the rear of the fighting and found shelter in the ruins of a farmhouse during the night. The next day we trudged through the falling snow, following the troops, and watched as the Brigade swept into the central square of Teruel. The Nationalists were in retreat. The men raised bloody fists into the air in celebration."*

I folded the thin pages of the letter and tucked them into my suitcase. I tried to imagine the snow-covered town square and the shivering but triumphant Spanish soldiers. Would the Republicans be able to hold Teruel when Franco sent more troops, planes and tanks to re-take the town? It was doubtful.

14
Barcelona
February, 1938

I crossed the frontier into Spain without hassles from the border officials. At both the French and Spanish checkpoints my documents were scrutinized carefully, but the Customs officers didn't even ask me to open my bags. Besides my suitcase of warm clothes I had brought an extra-large one filled with canned goods, smoked hams, whiskey, cigarettes and soap. Tom had mentioned in his letter the scarcity of these items, and I remembered Hemingway's larder in Madrid.

The train from Port Bou was almost empty. The conductor helped me lift my heavy bags up the steps of the train and place them on the floor of my compartment. I put my Corona portable on the seat beside me. I was the compartment's only occupant. My heart beat rapidly when we chugged out of the Port Bou railroad station. I felt a heightening of my senses, a tightening in my gut. I peered up at the starched blue sky, recalling the words of Josephine Herbst, but also remembering that cloudless skies could mean air attacks. I remained alert and watchful. I listened for the roar of airplane engines, but to my relief, all I heard were the clacking, metallic sounds of wheels on train tracks. As we approached Barcelona, I was dismayed to see that many of the factory buildings next to the tracks were piles of smashed red bricks and chunks of mortar. Women and children were poking into the ruins, scavenging.

My compartment had remained empty and very few passengers had climbed onto the train, but when I arrived in Barcelona, the platform was crowded with soldiers pushing their way onto a train on the opposite track. It would be going to Aragon, I guessed. I stood in the train corridor as it drew to a stop and scanned the crowd waiting on the platform. I wondered if Tom would be there to meet me. I had wired him my time of arrival.

I waited in the corridor a few moments, peering out the window, hoping to see Tom's tall figure lope down the platform, but he didn't appear. I was hit with a wave of disappointment, a sense of abandonment, of loss. I pulled my suitcase down from the rack and stared disconsolately at the heavy case at my feet. I would need help to move it. I descended the metal steps of the train, and set my one suitcase and typewriter on the sooty platform. As I searched the crowd for Tom—or at least for someone to help me drag out the food-laden bag I'd left in the compartment—I heard my name being called. My pulse quickened.

But it wasn't Tom rushing through the crowd. It was Ralph Fitzgerald. The brim of his brown fedora was pulled down so that I could only see the bottom edge of his horn-rimmed glasses, but I recognized him immediately. He gave me a bear hug that almost knocked me off my feet. "Meg, darling, you made it! I have a car for you. Tom arranged it."

"And Tom?" I asked. "Is he here?"

"No, he went to Teruel. The fighting is fierce again. Franco may re-take it. Everyone's there." He held me at arm's length. "But Meg, how are you? How was the trip? Let me help you with your bags." He pointed to my suitcase and typewriter case on the platform. "Is this all you brought?"

"No, I'll show you." We climbed into the train and Ralph lugged out my food-loaded bag and found a baggage cart. The car was waiting outside the station. I took in a breath of the chill Barcelona air. In both the train and the station the air had been stale and sooty, but here outside I could smell that dreaded combination of gunpowder and pulverized brick. Barcelona was taking a beating. The train station was intact, although the glass in several of the roof panels had shattered. The building next to it was missing the outside wall, the doll house effect I'd grown accustomed to in Madrid. I looked up at the sky, thankful for the thick fog that had blown in from the Mediterranean.

On the way to the hotel I bombarded Ralph with questions about the war and about Tom. Everyone had gone to the front, he'd said, but Tom would be careful. "He knows how to keep his head down, but it looks bad in Teruel. The Condor Legion is creating havoc, pounding the hell out of the Brigades. And most of us think it's likely the Nationalists will take back Teruel and win their drive to the sea."

"Ralph, what's so important about Teruel? Why did the Republicans choose to capture it? It's such a bleak, cold place—and a minor provincial town."

"Apparently intelligence was received that Franco was about to attack Guadalajara, north of Teruel, which is on the main road to Madrid. So the generals decided to mount at offensive against Teruel to draw off Franco's troops. They figured if the Republicans could hold that town, it would hinder Franco from taking Madrid—and Aragon—and reaching the Mediterranean.

"I see. And you, Ralph? You didn't go with the others to the front?"

"No, tomorrow I'm leaving Spain. The Trib's assigning me to Austria. There's a report that Hitler has positioned his troops at the Austrian border. My editor says Spain is a lost cause. His readers are no longer interested in what's happening here. Hitler may be on the move."

I felt as if the air had been punched out of my lungs. Was there no hope? I stared at Ralph, not wanting to believe his words.

Our driver skirted the bomb craters as he headed down the Ramblas, driving carefully over pulverized paving stones. The Majestic hotel was intact, but sandbags were stacked high against the walls, and the windows were boarded up or taped. When I walked through the door of the hotel, the lobby smelled musty, as if it hadn't been cleaned properly. It reminded me of the odor of the well-used lunch box I used to take to school as a child. Tom had told me the town had run out of soap, and it smelled like it.

A note from Tom was waiting for me at the desk. *Darling Meg, I'm so sorry I couldn't be at the train to meet you. The battle is raging around Teruel, and I had to go. Ralph promised he'd get you to the hotel and tell you all the dope. And congratulations on your promotion. But remember please, we're a TEAM. And I love you. I'll call the hotel as soon as I find a working phone. And stay safe. Air-raids have been bad. Ralph will show you the shelter. Got to go. TAKE CARE! Love, Tom*

Ralph helped carry my bags to my room. The men who had worked as porters were either at the front or working in Barcelona's underground factories. "Ralph, please stay a while. I brought some Scotch—and cigarettes. And are you hungry? I have some canned goods, too. You're looking thin."

He laughed. "I'm most certainly hungry. And I'm dying for a cigarette and I haven't had a Scotch since Hemingway left Madrid."

I took out the tiny luggage keys from my purse and unlocked the bag containing the precious supplies. I set the bottle of Scotch, the carton of cigarettes and a can of smoked oysters on the small table in the middle of the room. Ralph found two glasses by the washstand and fished out his fancy pocketknife to open the can. He quickly speared an oyster with the knife and I pried one up with a small fork I'd stashed with the food. I splashed some Scotch into the glasses and we toasted each other. "Salud!"

"Ralph, bring me up to date. So what's been happening while I've been gone that the censors won't let you write about?" I opened the carton of Galloises, peeled a pack open and offered him a cigarette.

"Christ, where to begin?" He lit both our cigarettes. "There's a lot of really bad stuff going on. We hear complaints about ammunition and supplies going only to the Communist-led troops. And the Communists are executing prisoners. Not only POUMistas, but Brigaders. This guy, Marty, the head Russian commissar? He suspects everyone of treason, of being a fascist spy. Prime Minister Negrín outlawed POUM and arrested headman, Nin. It's rumored Nin was tortured and killed." Ralph speared another oyster.

I felt a spiraling downward of my hopes for Spain. I'd never met Nin, but he had a reputation for being a brave fighter, loyal to the Republic and a deadly foe of fascism. How tragic that he would be tortured and killed by people fighting on the same side. I remembered Orwell's despair. I also recalled how I had refused to answer questions about Communist atrocities during my U.S. lectures.

Ralph took another gulp of Scotch. "And Hemingway's with the others at the front. Gellhorn's with him."

"And what about his Russian friend, Koltsov?"

"Koltsov was recalled to Moscow. So was General Goriev. Nobody has heard from them." Ralph knocked back the rest of his Scotch and I poured him another. His brown eyes were peering at me through his horn-rimmed glasses as he took another drink. "Nobody can figure out what the hell Stalin is up to!"

"Tom still admires him."

"He does, indeed." Ralph grinned. "And he bites my head off if I say anything against his hero." He stubbed out his cigarette and rose from the table. "Thanks for the treats, Meg. I'll let you unpack. Meet me later at the bar, OK? About seven?"

I nodded. "Good. And thanks for meeting my train."

"My pleasure!"

When I arrived at the bar that evening, instead of hearing the usual buzz of chatter among its occupants, I was confronted by a heavy silence. Ralph found me a seat, and noting what must have been my puzzled look, told me a report had just come through that the Nationalists had retaken Teruel. "Franco's offensive in Aragon has begun," he murmured.

A week after Ralph left Barcelona all the newspapers screamed the headline: Hitler marched into Austria—an act that became known as the Anschluss. The great dictator was on the move. Would the Western democracies never wake up?

15

Barcelona
March, 1938

For three weeks after I arrived in Barcelona the weather was unsettled. Rain fell frequently and the sky was dark with clouds, which meant that Nationalist planes could not fly. Relieved to be free from air-raids, Barcelonans were out on the streets, lining up at shops, grateful for the opportunity to purchase their meager daily ration of bread, rice or lentils.

Tom had not yet returned. In fact, most of the press corps was still in the field in Aragon and the news from the front was not good. Franco's troops were making headway toward the coast, which would cut Barcelona off from Madrid and Valencia. I had spoken to Tom a few times on the phone, but of necessity the calls were short. Reporters were queued up behind him, waiting to file their stories. Tom gave me brief accounts of what to write up for the news bureau at NBC in Paris. It was good to hear his voice, but frustrating not to be able to really talk to him. It was strange to be in Spain without him, but I was coping on my own quite well, I thought. And I had work to do.

Since the government had been moved from Valencia to Barcelona, I had hoped to find La Pasionaria in town. When I first called at her office I was told she was at the front in Aragon. She was one of the few women who were still welcome at the front.

I was at the railroad station interviewing two English Quaker women who were accompanying a group of twenty or so orphan children to England by way of France when I saw La Pasionaria hurrying toward us.

152

She waved, then abruptly stopped to speak to a little girl who was wiping her eyes on the cuff of her overly large coat. I watched as the black-clad woman patted the child's' cheek and then buttoned her coat tightly under her chin. The girl looked up at her with a bewildered gaze but had stopped crying. Dolores spoke softly to the child and then turned toward us. She shook hands with the two Quaker women. "I'd hoped to get here before you left. Is everything all arranged?"

"Dolores," I said, stepping forward, "how are you? I've been trying to find you, but they told me you were at the front."

"Margarita!" she cried, giving me a warm embrace. "You've returned! And I assume you're here at the station to write about our orphans and these brave English ladies."

"I am," I said, indicating my reporter's notebook.

She turned again to the women. "Your papers are all in order? The French consul stamped the children's transit visas?"

The women assured her in their English-accented Spanish that the documents had been signed by the Spanish, French and British officials. They then began helping the children up the steps of the carriage. A few seconds after the last child was helped onto the train, the conductor's whistle blew, the engine hissed and steamed, and the train began to move out of the station. We waved to the children peering out carriage windows, their eyes wide and solemn.

La Pasionaria sighed. "Poor things. They're all so thin. And most have rickets. This diet of lentils is disastrous for growing bones. Now we don't even have Valencia oranges. And so many more orphans. Over 2,000 here in Barcelona alone. We're trying to find places for them—America, England, France, Russia. But it takes time."

We emerged from the train station and Dolores led me toward a black Citroen. "Can I drop you somewhere. Your hotel?"

I accepted her offer and climbed into the back of the Citroen. As the young soldier driver dodged the piles of smashed bricks and stones, Dolores talked. When I asked her about Teruel and Aragon, her face darkened. "Not good. Not good at all. It's the leadership. Defense Minister Prieto provides his Socialist militias with arms, but the Communist-led troops receive almost nothing. Negrín must stop him!"

Ralph had told me that most complaints were the opposite, that the Communists were hogging the arms and ammunition. It was so absurdly tragic. Men were dying on the battlefield while their leaders fought viciously over the scarce supply of weapons.

La Pasionaria dropped me off at the hotel and I hurried to my room to type up my piece about the orphans. I preferred to use my own typewriter in my room rather than in the press room at Telefonica. My room was warmer. Although it was unheated, at least its glass windows were still intact, unlike the telephone building's smashed windows, which were covered with cardboard or old mattresses.

When I had finished typing I rushed over to Telefonica's censorship office where Catalina Rodriguez, a gaunt, nervous woman, would scan my story. I had met her in Madrid when she was one of Arturo Barea's switchboard censors. The censorship procedure was similar to the one I'd coped with in Madrid. I also asked her to censor the news items Tom had called in to me before I put in my call to the Paris office. Catalina quickly read my piece and Tom's news *snaps,* as these small pieces were called, and stamped it. She introduced me to the switchboard censor, a thin, bald man named Victor, who lifted his earphones from his head and shook my hand. Like his counterpart in Madrid I noted his fingernails were bitten to the quick.

When my call came through and I talked to Martin Bowen, at NBC Paris, his response to Tom's battle report was lukewarm. "We're covering the Anschluss story in Austria and the British-Italian pact. Chamberlain hopes Italy will be Britain's' ally in fighting Hitler when the war begins. Meg, our audience is losing interest in the fighting in Spain. But your orphan story should work. We'll set you up to broadcast tomorrow at 8PM. OK?"

The next day I woke to bright sunlight shining into my hotel room. The sky was a clear blue with not a cloud in sight. I knew the air-raids could begin again at any moment, and this time Tom wouldn't be at my side. I spent the day listening for airplanes, expecting the wail of the siren.

My broadcast went well, I thought. Victor, the switchboard censor, had left for home and I was in Catalina's office on the phone to Bowen in Paris when I heard the air-raid siren. I looked out the glassless window and spied the V formation of bombers, their wings glimmering in the light of the full moon. They were flying low, straight toward us. Catalina had stopped listening to my phone call and was peering through binoculars at the planes. "They're Italian. Savoias, I think!" She slammed down the glasses and grabbed her coat and purse. "Hurry. Downstairs. The shelter."

"It's an air-raid," I yelled into the phone. "Italian bombers!" I jammed the earpiece onto its hook and fled down the stairway. As my sturdy brogues clumped down the cement stairs, I flashed on the first air-raid I experienced in Madrid. I remembered the clatter of my high-heeled red shoes as I dashed down Telefonica's ten flights. Who was that girl? At that time my teeth chattered and my body trembled. Now I felt an adrenaline rush that propelled me rapidly downward. I was scared. My teeth were clamped tightly together to prevent their chattering, but I knew the routine. Ahead of me I caught a glimpse of Catalina, her brown coat billowing as she fled down the stairs.

I had almost caught up with her when a loud blast shook the building, knocking me against the inner wall of the stairway. I regained my balance, commanded my heart to stop racing, and continued to where Catalina lay sprawled on the stairs. She clutched at her ankle. "I twisted it," she moaned. I helped her to her feet and held onto her as she hobbled downward.

That night wave after wave of planes flew overhead. When we first heard the all-clear siren we decided to stay in the Telefonica cellar until morning. It was a fortunate decision, because about three hours later the warning siren wailed again. Once more we listened to the thud of bombs and hung on to our cots when the building shook. Cots, mattresses and blankets had been installed in the basement shelter.

At dawn when the all-clear sounded I ventured outside. Catalina hobbled at my side. Her ankle was painful and she needed my help to walk the two blocks to my hotel. I invited her to stay with me until she could find someone to take her to her apartment some distance away. The street was pocked with craters and littered with rubble. A building a block behind the hotel was in flames and the air was thick with smoke and soot. An ambulance careened by, zigzagging around the holes in the pavement, its siren howling its high and low lament.

When we entered our hotel, pale-faced residents were stumbling up from the basement where they had spent the night. Catalina and I took refuge in my room, hoping to catch some sleep. But that didn't happen.

By the time we had wrapped Catalina's ankle, and I had changed my clothes, the air-raid siren sounded again. I looked at my watch. Three hours had passed since the all-clear. Once more I grabbed my notebook, shoved a can of peaches and can opener in my purse, and helped Catalina down the stairs to the cellar shelter.

For the next two days the Italian Savoias dropped their bombs on the defenseless city. From our cellars we didn't know how they kept up this wave after wave of bombings. From what airfield were they launching the attack? Later we learned that they refueled and re-armed at their airfield on the island of Majorca in the Mediterranean—then returned to repeat the attack again and again. There were no anti-aircraft guns shielding Barcelona, and Republican fighter planes didn't scramble until the afternoon of the second day of bombings. At the press briefing the morning following the raids we heard what had happened. There had been seventeen raids. 1,300 civilians had been killed and more than 2,000 injured. The hospitals overflowed with wounded. Those of us who had cowered in the cellar at the Majestic were lucky. The hotel had not been hit and did not sustain serious damage during the explosions that occurred nearby. Once again my luck had held. But for how long?

As soon as the press briefing was over I went out onto the street to investigate the damage. I shoved my notebook in my coat pocket and hung my Leica around my neck. What we had experienced was the new type of warfare from the sky that targeted and destroyed helpless civilians, young and old. The world needed to learn about it and beware.

What I witnessed was heartbreaking. My jaw firmly clenched, I watched two soldiers dig out a bloodied old woman from beneath a pile of bricks and stone and then carry her on a stretcher to the ambulance parked in the middle of the street. She was unconscious, the soldier said. I wondered if she would survive. My hands were shaking, but with icy fingers I set the aperture of my camera, steadied the camera against my face and clicked the shutter as the soldiers lifted the stretcher into the vehicle. I was working automatically, numbly. Would this woman be counted as one of the injured, I wondered? Number 1,301? Or of the dead, 1001? The ambulance drove off and the soldiers moved to the next wrecked building.

I picked my way through the red brick dust and debris to the plaza and snapped images of the blackened, destroyed buildings around it. The air was dense with smoke and cement dust. It was difficult to breathe. Ambulance sirens shrieked, cars lumbered through the cratered square, men and women lifted bricks and rubble with their hands crying out to the trapped people beneath. The scorched body of a dead cat lay across the pavement. I let my camera drop on its strap around my neck and turned my back on the scene. There was only so much I could take.

That evening I heard a radio report that Mussolini and Italian Foreign Minister, Count Ciano, were delighted with the damage their bombs had inflicted on Barcelona. Then I wept.

That night after the bombing I was awakened from a deep sleep by the sound of knocking on my door. At first I thought I was dreaming and buried my head in my pillow. The knocking continued, becoming more persistent. I sat up and lit the candle on my bedside table. Then I heard a low voice calling my name—a familiar voice. Suddenly wide-awake, I snatched up my robe and unlocked the door. Tom rushed into the room, picked me up, twirled me around and kissed me hard. His chin was rough with a blond stubble, and his coat was spattered with mud. He smelled of sweat and mud, a ripe male smell. Laughing, I pulled away and closed the door and locked it. We stood in the middle of the room staring at each other.

"God, I'm glad you're safe, Meg. I heard about the bombing and was scared to death you might have been hit." He hugged me tightly. I closed my eyes, savoring the sense of safety. I then leaned back and stared into his face, which was lit by the flickering flame of the candle. His eyes were red with lack of sleep and encircled with black and his face was spattered with mud, but he still exuded energy. He gave me an intense look and fished a key out of his coat pocket. "I have the room down the hall. The night clerk said he'd find my bag I'd checked when I left for Aragon. He'll take it to my room—but Meg, I want to stay right here—with you. In this room. In your bed."

His look was disarming, expectant. I found myself thinking how easy it would be to jump into bed with him, but did I really want to? I'd expected to have time to consider if we should continue our affair. "So you think we can start up again where we left off six months ago?"

He placed both his hands on my face, his deep blue eyes fixed on mine. "Oh yes, Meg. You're here. Now. And I love you! "

I hadn't said either yes or no, but he was persuasive. And tomorrow we could be hit by bullets or shrapnel or the building could be hit by a bomb and collapse on top of us. So why worry about the future? I gave him a mischievous smile, glanced at the bed and then at his grubby form.

He grinned and peered down at his muddy coat and shoes. He pointed to his rucksack he'd dumped by the door. "All the stuff I took with me is filthy but I'll go get my other suitcase and take a bath."

"Tom, there's no hot water and no electricity, but I can heat some up on the spirit stove. And I have soap!" I disentangled myself, filled a kettle with water and lit the stove. He stripped off his muddy coat, tossed it on a chair, then sank wearily on the edge of the bed. "I saw the ruins on the streets as I rode into town. Those bastards! But, Meg, you're OK? The hotel wasn't hit?"

"No. I have a shattered window pane." I pulled aside the blackout curtain to show him the cardboard that had been tacked over it. "And we spent three days in the basement shelters. But what about Aragon? Is it as bad as I've heard?"

"It's horrible. A bloody hell. A fucking disaster."

I sat next to him and leaned close. "Barcelona, too. A bloody hell." His arms wrapped around me and I knew I wanted him to stay.

So Tom and I were lovers again. Our working relationship had changed, but we were both so concerned about the conditions in the city and the people around us, we didn't have time to consider how it would affect us. After being separated for six months the first few days of the resumption of our affair was like a honeymoon.

We also talked, of course. We talked a lot. We had much to catch up on and at first we had few disagreements. Tom was dismayed at the destruction he saw on the streets. "It's not only the docks they're targeting, but also the workers' neighborhoods. Innocent civilians," he fumed. Luckily, that first day rain was pounding the city and neither German nor Italians planes could fly. At the press briefing Catalina announced a piece of good news—for a change. "Prime Minister Negrín has persuaded the French to open the frontier to Spain for shipments of armaments. He flew to Paris last week to speak to Blum." Blum was a Socialist, like Negrin, and had just become Prime Minister. Hearing that news was like a pinpoint of sunshine glimmering through dark clouds.

After the briefing Tom and I took shelter at a cellar bar, Miguel's, to avoid the drenching rain. Miguel's hadn't been damaged in the bombings and still served brandy or wine. No tapas, of course. Our diet consisted of lentil soup and a rare piece of bread. Anthony Thomas was sitting at a candle-lit table in the corner and beckoned to us to join him. "So, Tom, you're back from the front. And all in one piece." They shook hands. "And Meg, you're looking well." He arched his eyebrows. "You're still hooked up with this bloke!"

I nodded, but refrained from saying what I was thinking—that we were together at least for the moment. Tom called to the waiter and ordered wine, which he quickly served. "Salud," Tom said, leaning back in his chair, sipping the wine. "Anthony, I didn't see you at the briefing. Did you hear the good news?"

"About the French opening the frontier for shipments of arms? Yes, I was at the Ministry earlier. But have you heard that Prieto's calling for peace negotiations?"

Tom scowled. His blue eyes eyes sparked. "That defeatist! No, I hadn't. I don't understand why Negrin doesn't get rid of him." He slammed down his wine glass and drops of the red liquid splashed onto the table.

I stared at him. Why was he so adamant in his distrust of Prieto? I remembered the conversation I had with La Pasionaria about Prieto. She'd also used the term defeatist. From what I had gleaned from other reporters, Socialist Prieto believed the Republic could avoid complete defeat by beginning negotiations with Franco. The Communists strongly disagreed. Tom was sticking to the Stalinist line again. He hadn't changed. A queasy feeling crept into my gut. How could he still believe in Stalin after knowing about the show trials in Moscow and the Stalinists' summary executions and secret prisons here in Spain?

I refrained from talking about the peace negotiations with Tom. I didn't want our quarrels to begin again and I knew he would soon be leaving for the front. Fighting had become fierce and the Nationalists had almost reached the Mediterranean. When Tom left I was on my own again. I concentrated on my work. The weather cleared and Barcelona suffered more bombings. The bomb explosions shook the basement shelters of the Majestic or Telefonica, where I huddled in fear. It was impossible to sleep and I was always exhausted. The reporters who remained in town bolstered my courage. They were a lively lot, and tried to keep up a stream of jokes—gallows humor. Occasionally one of them would make a pass at me, but wasn't offended when I refused his attentions. For the moment I had committed myself to Tom.

And I didn't have time to ponder. The wounded Brigaders were brought into the local hospitals and billeted in the basements, where they lay on the floor or the stretchers on which they had been carried. I wrote letters for wounded American and Canadian Brigaders and sometimes admired the crumpled photographs of girlfriends, wives or mothers they carried in their wallets. I typed up my pieces in my room or in the shelters during bombing raids.

One of the soldiers I visited, an English-speaking Italian, who was recuperating from a bullet wound in his shoulder, told me he had been a journalist for a leftist Milanese newspaper. "When Mussolini came to power I was arrested, thrown into jail and given the caster oil treatment."

"For working for a leftist paper?"

"I was accused of being a Communist spy. I was sure I would be sent to one of Mussolini's notorious prisons—like the guys who were picked up at the same time I was. One of the guards was a cousin of my sister's husband and helped me escape from the jail. I got to France and joined the International Brigade." His green-gold eyes were rimmed with thick black lashes and when he smiled his face lit up. His name was Gino Baroli. I visited him every day for two weeks. He wrote down my name and we promised to meet somehow when the war was over.

Tom called in his news *snaps* to Telefonica and I wrote them up as well as my own pieces for Catalina to censor. Miraculously, the telephone system still functioned. While Tom was at the front Catalina announced that Prieto had resigned as War Minister. It was a relief, in a way, to hear that news while Tom was away. I knew we would have quarreled had we been together. About two weeks later Catalina read us the report that the Nationalists had taken the town of Vinaroz on the Mediterranean. Barcelona was now cut off from both Madrid and Valencia. It was bad news, indeed, a disastrous defeat. When I heard the report I was shaken. Now our only escape from Spain through Republican-held territory was the narrow corridor to the French border along the coast. It was no longer possible to go by sea from Barcelona. Ships were being sunk by Italian submarines or bombed from the air. Would Franco consider me a Communist spy and throw me in prison or march me to the firing squad?

Tom hadn't called in that day with his news and I was alarmed. How would he get back to Barcelona? When I went into one of the hospitals to interview soldiers, I could envision Tom on one of those stretchers. It took Tom three days to return to Barcelona. "Four of the guys and I finally got a ride in a truck that took the route north of Vinaroz up the coast road," he said, his face drawn and white with exhaustion.

Tom's return from the Aragon was a more intense repeat of his first re-entry into my life. We were very much aware of the disaster confronting us. Every moment could be our last. Tom remained in Barcelona three days and was off again—to the battle of the Ebro, a river in the north, which turned out to be the last big fight between the Nationalists and Republican forces. The Nationalists' superior air power won the battle—after huge loss of lives on both sides. Franco was winning.

Many journalists were leaving Spain. Anthony was sent to Czechoslovakia, where Hitler's troops were poised for possible invasion. He and Ralph Fitzgerald had been my companions since after first arriving in Spain. I missed them both. I had made friends with another journalist, Jerry Miller, whom I had met on the drive from Valencia to Barcelona with Ralph and Mountie. Jerry, a sidekick of Herbert Matthews, reporter for the NY Times, was from Boston. He was only a few years older than I and had a quirky sense of humor. I had learned how to take my place as one of the boys without Tom being at my side. Living in constant danger of being blown up by bombs or hit by shrapnel, we of the Barcelona press corps were comrades in arms.

These last few depressing months of the war were like a descent into hell. The bombings continued and hordes of displaced people trudged into the city looking for shelter that didn't exist. On my dashes to the press office between air-raids I could barely keep back my tears as I eyed soldiers from the Brigades wounded at the Ebro limping into town on makeshift crutches, helped by bandaged companions. The hospitals overflowed with victims, both civilian and military. People were starving. I saw women faint from hunger while standing in line for their meager ration of lentils.

And the bad news piled higher and higher. At a press briefing Catalina announced that the border to Spain for shipments of arms and ammunition had been closed. "Blum is no longer Prime Minister. Deladier is back in power." Then she told us about the Munich Pact. "Neville Chamberlain and Deladier have pressured the Czechs to cede the Sudetenland to Germany. England and France have appeased Hitler." I felt as if I were sinking into the deepest rings of hell. It was clear the war in Spain would soon be over. I didn't doubt that all Europe would soon be in flames. Hitler and fascism would not be stopped. I felt gripped by some incapacitating disease.

A week or so later Jerry Miller returned from Prague, where he had covered the Sudetenland story. Over drinks at Miguel's he told me what he had witnessed in Vienna where he had stopped on his return to Barcelona. His story reinforced my sense of being overtaken by a horrifying plague. "Brown shirted SA patrols and gangs of Nazi youths swooped through the streets," Jerry said, "burning synagogues, smashing Jewish shops, beating Jews in their homes. It continued for two days. The air was filled with smoke and the sidewalks were covered in broken glass. When it was over I interviewed a twelve-year old boy, the nephew of a friend of mine. He told me how he and his mother had ridden streetcars all of the second day of the raids to avoid the gangs. He had held a package on his lap as if he were headed for a birthday party."

Jerry's mouth had tightened as he spoke. He then gulped down his wine and poured another glass. "Apparently, the identical scene was happening all over Germany, Austria and the Sudetenland. The raids were superbly organized—supposedly in retaliation for the assassination by a Jewish boy of a German diplomat in Paris. I saw Austrian police arresting Jewish men on the street and dragging them away. Each man had to show the police his identity card. If it was marked with a J he was arrested."

I stared at Jerry, astonished. His story was painful, difficult to believe, but I knew it was true. And the nightmare continued. The bad news didn't stop. Two weeks later, Negrin announced that the

International Brigades would be withdrawn from Spain. Tom returned from the Ebro, his eyes expressionless. He fell onto the bed and slept for twelve hours. The next day we received a wire from NBC Paris. *You are both to leave Spain for France as soon as the International Brigades depart. Call from Perpignan for your next assignments. Martin Bowen, Paris bureau chief.*

As the International Brigades marched by the reviewing stand on this day at the end of November, 1938, the Chato fighters flying in the blue sky above dipped their wings in salute. Tears flowed down cheeks of the hundreds of Barcelonans who gathered to wave and throw flowers to the departing soldiers. Many of the soldiers also wept. I felt my heart would break as I eyed their faces, the worn and dirty uniforms that hung on the gaunt bodies of these brave men. I couldn't stop my tears. I glanced at Tom, who stood at my side, his expression one of shock and disbelief.

The officer ordered the soldiers to halt while Prime Minister Negrin approached the microphone and expressed his thanks to the foreigners who had come to the aid of the Republic. He then introduced La Pasionaria. The crowd fell silent. She stood before the microphone and surveyed the gathering. I was close enough to see the pain in her eyes. "Mothers! Women! When the years pass by and the wounds of war are staunched; when the cloudy memory of the sorrowful, bloody days returns in a present of freedom, love and well-being; when the feelings of rancor are dying away and when pride in a free country is felt equally by all Spaniards—then speak to your children. Tell them of the International Brigades. Tell them how, coming over seas and mountains, crossing frontiers bristling with bayonets and watched for by ravening dogs thirsty to tear at their flesh, these men reached our country as Crusaders for freedom. They gave up everything, their homes, their country, home and fortune—fathers, mothers wives, brothers, sisters and children, and they came and told us: 'We are here, your cause, Spain's cause, is ours. It is the cause of all advanced and progressive mankind.' Today they are going away. Many of them, thousands of them, are staying here with the Spanish earth for their shroud, and all Spaniards remember them with the deepest feeling." She then focused her eyes on the soldiers standing at attention in front of the reviewing stand. "Comrades of the International Brigades! Political reasons, reasons of State, the welfare of that same cause for which you offered your blood with boundless generosity, are sending you back, some of you to your own countries and others to forced exile. You can go proudly. You are history. You are legend. You are the heroic example of democracy's solidarity and universality. We shall not forget you, and when the olive tree of peace puts forth its leaves again, mingled with the laurels of the Spanish republic's victory—come back!"

After several seconds of silence, broken only by the sounds of sobs, the crowd let forth a roar of approval. Tears flowed as they shouted. The band struck up the *Internationale*, which the men began to sing in a multitude of languages. The parade moved on. Tom and I were standing with what remained of the press corps. After mopping my face with a sodden handkerchief I glanced at my colleagues. At least half of these hard-bitten, cynical reporters were wiping tears from their eyes. Tom was still dry-eyed. I linked my arm in his but didn't speak.

The Brigades were moving along the street quite smartly now. Suddenly, I spied my Italian friend, Gino Baroli, marching by, his arm in a sling. I called out to him and waved. He turned his head and our eyes connected. He smiled and lifted his chin in a silent greeting. Tom gave me a questioning look. "One of your wounded?"

I nodded. "An Italian anti-fascist. Escaped from a prison in Milan." What will he do now, I wondered? Will the French accept him? He can't return to Italy. He'd be thrown in some miserable prison—or be shot.

The parade ended, the officials on the reviewing stand climbed into the black cars and moved down the street, and we maneuvered through the crowd toward the Ministry where Catalina would be giving a press briefing—my last one here in Spain. Tom and I would be leaving the next day on the train for France. I looked up at the blue sky, wondering why the German and Italian bombers were not flying this day, "The bombers stayed away," I said to Tom, who was scribbling in his notebook.

"Yeah. They didn't want to interrupt the wonderful exit scene." His tone was sarcastic, angry.

After the press briefing, at which Catalina had given us copies of La Pasionaria's speech, we stopped in at Miguel's for a drink. The bar was crowded but we found a table in the corner. Jerry Miller and a British journalist, Alistair Field soon joined us.

We all ordered Spanish brandy. "Salud!" we said, almost in unison. "Blimey," said Field, "what a scene—and what a speech. The old girl was downright eloquent."

"Sad," Jerry responded quietly. "What was Negrin thinking of? Did he really believe the Germans and Italians would withdraw their troops as soon as the foreigners in the Brigades were pulled out?"

Tom gulped down his brandy and ordered another for all of us. His eyes sparked with anger. "Negrin should be fired—pronto. What sort of naïve idiot would go to the League of Nations and give the speech he did? Those diplomats are out of their minds! Nitwits. And that bastard, Chamberlain. Appeasement of Hitler! Chamberlain has to be stark raving mad! Does he truly believe he can avoid war? He's a fascist in sheep's clothing, that's what he is. And Deladier's no better."

Jerry sipped his brandy, eying Tom over the rim of his glass. "The Russians are pulling out, you know, Tom. Most of their people have been recalled to Moscow. Goriev and Koltsov were arrested there. Just like so many others. I heard it from Ehrenburg, the Tass correspondent. Off the record, of course. And I'd bet Koltsov and Goriev have been shot or sent to Siberia. Stalin's official line is no longer anti-fascist. He's buddying up with Hitler against the West."

Field fished out a crumpled pack of Galoises from his jacket pocket. "It's obvious Chamberlain hopes Germany and Italy will attack Russia, but who knows what Stalin will do? He's the craziest of the lot!"

I shot a look at Tom. His neck had become flushed and his jaw clenched. "Stalin knows what he's doing, Field!" He tossed some pesetas on the table and touched my arm. "Let's go, Meg." He turned on his heel and herded me out the door.

Our last night in Spain together was a disaster. I had been shocked to hear about Stalin's toadying to Hitler—and Koltsov's and General Goriev's arrest. To me it was beyond comprehension. "Tom, I just don't understand! Stalin must truly be out of his mind!"

Tom's face was dark with anger. "Meg, you don't know what you're talking about," he snapped. "You're politically naïve. You believe the lies they tell about Stalin. They create those stories of executions and exile to paint Stalin as a monster. And to make villains out of Communists.

It's all lies. And Stalin's toadying to Hitler, as you call it, is his strategy to give him time to prepare for war with Germany. He's no fool. You're a typical wishy-washy American Liberal!"

I was stunned by his words. I exploded. "Tom, you're blind. You've swallowed their propaganda. You must know that Stalin is another tyrant! He's controlling his Party with brute terror. His secret police are ruthless. I've been sickened by what they've done—the terror, the killings. And you, Tom, you don't give a damn about Koltsov or Goriev and how they fought for Republican Spain. You close your eyes to Marty's summary executions of our own soldiers of the International Brigade. Men who've risked their lives!" I found myself shouting at Tom. Angry words spilled from my mouth. Words I had locked up for weeks.

He shouted back. "It's the end that matters. Not the means. Reactionary spies deserve to be executed. You've got to be tough!" He strode out the door of my room and slammed it behind him. Outraged tears were welling in my eyes, but I shook them away and began to throw clothes into my suitcase. I'd had it. Tom and I were through. I didn't like who he had become. That last night in Spain I slept in my bed alone.

The train to the frontier from Barcelona was jammed with soldiers. I was squeezed between Tom and Field. Tom and I had barely talked to each other since the evening before. Tom was still scowling. He muttered Negrin's name to Field, cursing Negrin for his stupidity, for withdrawing the Brigades, for sucking up to the League of nitwits. I wasn't listening.

I was watching the soldiers surrounding us. The men in our car were French. They slouched on the seats and floors of the compartments or slumped against the walls of the corridors. A few slept, their heads on their packs. Others stared numbly out the window at their last glimpse of Spain. Hardly anyone spoke. Some had tears in their eyes. I thought about La Pasionaria's speech. Were these men thinking of their comrades buried in Spanish earth? Did they feel they were abandoning Spain and its people to the tyrant, Franco? I fixed my eyes on the soldiers by the window and the passing Spanish landscape. My heart was breaking.

16
France
November, 1938

The three of us, Field, Tom and I, crossed from Spain into France in the midst of columns of soldiers. When I stepped through the Spanish barrier gate into *no mans land* between the two countries, I felt a terrible sense of loss and guilt—as if I were abandoning the people I had come to love and respect. It seemed certain Franco would win. What would happen to the loyal people of Madrid, Barcelona, and the Aragon? Would the brave-hearted Spanish soldiers be slaughtered when they surrendered as had happened in Badajoz?

The Brigaders around me shuffled as they walked. A chill wind blew from the sea. They shivered with cold, their shoulders stooped. The French Brigaders were met by an officer who lined them up and marched them to a waiting train headed for Paris. A row of trucks was parked next to the French frontier, their engines running. Brigade officers were shouting out orders in a myriad of languages, assembling the men into their national groups: British, American, Canadian, Swiss, Belgian, Swedes, Poles. Men with armbands stating they were from the League of Nations strutted about importantly like roosters in a barnyard. Tom eyed them with contempt. He then hurried ahead, hoping to find a taxi to drive the three of us to Perpignan.

I caught sight of my Italian friend, Gino Baroli. His left arm was still in a sling. He was trudging toward a crowd of soldiers who had been called together by a trio of officials. One of the officials wore a League armband. I speculated the soldiers being assembled would be the men who could not return to their home countries: the German Jews or Communists, the Austrians, Italians, Czechs. I called out to Gino. He turned, recognized me, and shouldered through the jumble of soldiers to my side. I shook his free hand and introduced him to Field, summarizing Baroli's situation. "So, Gino, what's the story? What happens now? Will the French allow you to stay? Will the League help you obtain documents?"

Gino shrugged, his expression one of despair. "I don't know yet, but knowing French officials—and the League of Nations—it won't be soon."

I was witnessing the cruelty of the bureaucratic national laws that insisted upon passports and visas and special permits to enter or leave their countries. These border police and bureaucrats had the power of life or death. They could insist the men return to their own countries— where they would be killed or thrown into a concentration camp. "Is there anything we can do to help?"

Baroli gave a wry laugh. "How about a visa to the United States!"

I gave him a sad shake of my head. "Not unless you know someone influential—and even then ..." My voice failed me. "How about you, Alistair? Any ideas?"

He hesitated a moment, fixing his gray eyes on Gino. "We could try publicizing your plight. It might help. But don't get your hopes up. I'll talk to my editor. Our paper champions leftist causes." He pulled out his notebook and scribbled some notes. I did the same. Field gave Baroli a scrutinizing look. "Your English is good. You're a journalist? What paper did you write for?"

"*Il Giorno Milanese*. For three years. My beat was syndicate news."

Field and I exchanged glances. I shoved my notebook into my pocket. "Gino, maybe we can help you find a job. Then they might give you a visa. We can try, anyway."

He thanked us profusely, shook Field's hand, then grasped mine. "Margarita, where can I reach you?"

"The NBC news bureau—in Paris, London or New York. I don't know yet where I'll be sent. But they'd know." Gino kissed me on both cheeks and hurried off to join his battalion. Before he disappeared into the lineup of fellow soldiers he turned and waved, "arrivederci!"

A few moments later Tom returned with a beat-up Citroen taxi and a huge sack of croissants. "Look!" he shouted. "Food!" He spoke with his mouth full and passed the sack under our noses. We all munched on croissants as we hauled our suitcases and typewriters into the taxi. As I stood by the car, I glanced at the soldiers clambering into the trucks, searching for Gino, knowing he would be hungry, wondering if I could get some food to him. "I wonder if we can find out where these undocumented men will be billeted while they wait for their papers."

"It shouldn't be too difficult," Tom said. He stopped loading our bags and stared at the soldiers as they climbed wordlessly into the trucks. "Poor screwed heroes!" Tom's angry frown disappeared. Now I could see the sorrow in his eyes as he surveyed the scene before him. Had he stopped obsessing about Negrin and the Socialists? Was he reverting to the Tom I once thought I knew, the compassionate, rational journalist?

Abruptly, he turned and faced the frontier. He took hold of my hand and drew me toward the barrier that served as the French border. A few feet beyond lay the Spanish barrier. "Our last glimpse of Spain," Tom murmured.

I gazed up at the Republican flag that flapped above the Spanish police shelter, certain I would never see it again. Tears welled in my eyes. Then I heard the taxi driver calling to us. Still holding hands, Tom and I numbly turned our backs on the country we had learned to love and climbed silently into the Citroen.

The road to Perpignan ran along the coast for about forty kilometers. Our taxi driver drove slowly, trapped in the convoy of the trucks carrying Brigade soldiers. At Cerbére, a beach town ten kilometers or so from the frontier, three of the trucks had stopped. Men were unloading their gear. "It looks like they're setting up camp," Tom said. "Right on the beach."

I craned my neck as we passed, hoping to catch sight of Gino among the soldiers jumping down from the truck beds, but I didn't see him.

Field pulled out his notebook. "I think those are the blokes who can't go home," he said, jotting down the name of the town. Tom and I did the same.

"A detention camp?" I said. "Poor souls." Poor Gino, I thought.

It took an hour to drive to Perpignan. We spoke very little. The chaos we had witnessed had been too disturbing. I felt impotent, hollow, and glancing at Tom and Field, I speculated they felt the same. Insanely, I wanted to return to Spain, to man the barricades, which wasn't my job, of course. Instead, I vowed, I would write about the stateless International Brigade soldiers. But where would I be sent next? Would Martin, the Paris bureau chief, permit me to stay here a few days to investigate?

I shot a glance at Tom. He was staring out the window, his expression one of defeat and melancholy. What would be his next assignment, I wondered. Where would Martin send him? I was almost certain we would not be together. Tonight we must talk. And go our separate ways?

Our driver dropped us at the Grand Hotel. We booked two rooms. Tom and Field would double up and I was given a small room on the third floor. We asked about phoning to Paris and the concierge pointed to the telephone room where we could place our calls. He told us it might take a few hours to get an open line. "The League officials and consuls are making arrangements for the International Brigades. Alors! Talk, talk talk!"

We quickly settled into our rooms and then returned to the lobby to book our calls. Until we spoke to Martin in Paris, we could make no plans. Tom and I waited at a corner table at the bar for our calls to come through. We didn't mention our quarrel or politics or what we'd seen at the frontier. We were in a kind of limbo. Neither of us wanted a confrontation. We stuck to small talk. "I can hardly wait for dinner," I said lightly, sipping my glass of the local white wine.

Tom smiled, the first smile I'd seen him give for days. "I'm thinking about foie gras, steak, pomme frites, a plate of cheeses!"

I laughed. "Please, Tom. Don't." I glanced at my watch. "We have another two hours before they serve dinner."

We continued this type of inane banter until the telephone operator called our names. We dashed to the phones. Tom spoke first. He listened without speaking for a long moment, shot me a glance, then said, "Prague. OK. I'll leave here tomorrow."

He handed me the phone and Martin told me my assignment was London, that I should proceed to Paris for my papers. "Martin, there's a great story I'd like to do here—about the stateless soldiers of the International Brigade. They're camped on the beach. It shouldn't take me long. A friend of mine is among them. I could come to Paris next week."

"OK, Meg. Good idea. And check out the Abraham Lincoln Brigade. See you next week."

I set down the phone and eyed Tom, who was staring at me. "So what's your assignment?" he said, his face a mask.

"London. But I'll stay here this week."

"I heard. And you want to do a story about your Italian friend."

"Yes. And you're going to Prague. Leaving tomorrow."

Tom nodded still staring at me. "First I go to Paris for my German and Czech visas." He paused. "And you won't be coming with me. No last night in Paris."

"Right." My throat felt constricted. We moved toward our table at the bar. "Tom we've got to talk."

"Yeah," he said, taking a deep breath. And I think I know what you're going to say—but let's go up to your room."

The day I left Spain was the last day of my love affair with Tom Wells. Sadly, we agreed to go our separate ways. The next day Tom left for Paris and then Prague, where four months later he witnessed Hitler's troops invade Czechoslovakia. I was in London when Franco marched into Madrid in March of '39. Tom phoned the London bureau that day, guessing that I would be glued to the teletype machine. We spoke through our tears.

When Hitler began bombing Poland, and Britain and France responded by declaring war on Germany, I didn't have time to worry about Tom. The war that we all knew would envelope the world had begun. I didn't see him again until after Hitler had occupied France in June of 1940 and initiated the blitz in England. Tom barged into the London bureau to report on his coverage of the evacuation of British troops from Dunkirk. I was in the studio during his broadcast. His description of the heroic civilians in small boats facing enemy fire to rescue the soldiers was powerful, indeed. He was a damned good journalist. We went out to dinner after his broadcast, and a frisson of electricity still flowed between us. He hadn't changed, was as good looking as ever, and exuded energy, but to my amazement he still made excuses for Stalin's "alleged" tyranny. I never saw him again, but I knew he continued being a war correspondent. As the years went by I'd hear his radio dispatches from some corner of the world where a war was waging—and tragically there was no dearth of these.

And my story? Just before D-day I met an American army officer in London, a lawyer from San Francisco, and we fell in love. We were married, had two sons, and I continued to work in broadcasting until I got a teaching job at the U.C. Berkeley Journalism school. We have a happy marriage, but from time to time I feel a twinge of nostalgia for those dramatic days—and nights—in Spain so long ago.

Tom Wells remained in my memory along with the men and women I met there. And I'll never forget that heartbreaking moment when we realized Franco would win the war and plunge the country into darkness. We had to wait a long time for Franco to die and for the Spanish people to become free again. Viva España!

NOTE

When Franco declared victory and the civil war ended many Spaniards escaped to France. The French forced many into detention camps. When the Germans invaded France they turned over the Spanish former soldiers to Franco, where they were executed. Franco ordered the execution of over 150,000 Spaniards after the war.

La Pasionaria escaped from Spain by air to Algiers and then to Moscow a few days before the Republic surrendered to Franco. Her son was killed in the defense of Stalingrad, but she survived. She did not return to Madrid until 1977 when she was elected deputy for parliament from Asturias, the position she held during the civil war. The monarchy had been restored, and King Juan Carlos had set the stage for the election of a parliamentary government.

When WWII ended, it was confirmed that Koltsov, General Goriev, Grigorovitch, the tank commander, Pavlov and several others who had fought in Spain were all shot at Stalin's orders. Orlov, the Russian NKVD spy, defected to Canada in July of 1938. He lived in the the U.S and assisted the FBI in certain cases of espionage.

Arthur Koestler spent several months in Franco's prison in Malaga under a death sentence, but was released through the efforts made by the British. Koestler, Orwell and Dos Passos turned against the Communist Party. Although Koestler and Orwell remained leftists, Dos Passos became a political conservative after his experience in Spain. It was said that the bullet that killed Jose Robles killed any sympathy Dos Passos held for the communists.

Bibliography

Barea, Arturo, *The Forging of a Rebel,* Walker and Co, N.Y,2001.

Beevor, Antony, *The Spanish Civil War,* Penguin Books, N.Y., 2001.

Brookchin, Murray, *To Remember Spain, The Anarchist and Syndicalist Revolution of 1936.* AK, San Francisco, 1994.

Hellman, Lilian, *Three, An Unfinished Woman,* Little Brown and Co. Boston, 1979.

Ibarruri, Dolores, *They Shall Not Pass, the Autobiography of La Pasionaria,* International Publishers, 1976.

Stephen Koch, *The Breaking Point, Hemingway, Dos Passos and the murder of Jose Robles,* Counterpoint, 2005.

Koestler, Arthur, *Dialogue With Death,* Macmillan Co. New York, 1960.

Langor, Elinor, *Josephine Herbst, the story she could never tell.* Warner Books, New York, 1985.

Ehrenberg, Ilya, *Memoirs, 1921-1941,* London, 1963.

Orwell, George, *Homage to Catalonia,* Harcourt Brace & Co. 1952.

Phillips, C.E. Lucas, *The Spanish Pimpernel,* William Heinemann Ltd, London, 1960.

Regler, Gustav, *The Owl of Minerva, the autobiography of Gustav Regler,* Rupert Hart-Davis, London, 1959.

Rollyson, Carl, *Beautiful Exile, the life of Martha Gellhorn,* Aurum Press, London, 2001.

Thomas, Hugh, *The Spanish Civil War,* Modern Library, New York, 2001.